2 7

... The table rattled with the force of
Leah's movement.

"This is the only way I will even consider your
request."

"What do you expect me to do for these three
months?"

"Convince me that you're serious about
this fashion design career—that you won't
drain your inheritance on some trumped-up
business."

"The vote of confidence in your tone is *really*
inspiring."

The hardness in his eyes didn't budge. "I'm
giving you a real choice. If you fail, our
marriage stands. You'll be my wife in every
sense—for as long as one of us is alive."

Greek Tycoons Tamed

When power and pride are undone by passion!

Stavros Sporades and Dmitri Karegas
are renowned throughout the world as
Greece's most powerful and determined tycoons!

But have these untouchable Greek tycoons
finally met the women who can tame them?

Find out in…

Stavros and Leah's story:

Claimed for His Duty

August 2015

The wife Stavros hasn't seen for nearly five years
is back and demanding a divorce! But Stavros
isn't about to let his errant wife escape from his grasp…
they have unfinished business!

Dmitri and Jasmine's story:

Bought for Her Innocence

November 2015

Dmitri is known for the women who visit his bed
as much as for the millions in his bank account.
So when a childhood friend auctions her innocence
Dmitri intends to be the highest bidder!

CLAIMED FOR HIS DUTY

BY
TARA PAMMI

Published in Great Britain 2015
by Mills & Boon, an imprint of Harlequin (UK) Limited,
Eton House, 18-24 Paradise Road, Richmond, Surrey, TW9 1SR

© 2015 Tara Pammi

ISBN: 978-0-263-24900-2

Harlequin (UK) Limited's policy is to use papers that are natural, renewable and recyclable products and made from wood grown in sustainable forests. The logging and manufacturing processes conform to the legal environmental regulations of the country of origin.

Printed and bound in Spain
by CPI, Barcelona

Tara Pammi can't remember a moment when she wasn't lost in a book—especially a romance, which was much more exciting than a mathematics textbook. Years later, Tara's wild imagination and love for the written word revealed what she really wanted to do. Now she pairs Alpha males who think they know everything with strong women who knock that theory *and* them off their feet!

Books by Tara Pammi

Mills & Boon® Modern™ Romance

The Man to Be Reckoned With
A Deal with Demakis

Society Weddings

The Sicilian's Surprise Wife

A Dynasty of Sand and Scandal

The Last Prince of Dahaar
The True King of Dahaar

The Sensational Stanton Sisters

A Hint of Scandal
A Touch of Temptation

**Visit the author profile page at
millsandboon.co.uk for more titles**

CHAPTER ONE

LEAH HUNTINGTON COLLAPSED onto the plastic chair behind her small desk, her knees buckling out from under her. The red stamp spelling out "REJECTED" on the application form blurred in front of her eyes. Her heart squeezed painfully as she fingered the flat sketches on her drawing board, the possibility of seeing her creation take form now evaporating like a puff of smoke.

Sweat ran down her back, the slow whir of the ceiling fan scraping against her nerves. She ran cramped up fingers over her neck, feeling the muscles tighten with tension.

Mrs. DuPont, the buying manager for a retail store, had given Leah only two months to create her first collection and all Leah had now were flat sketches. And as she had to do everything herself instead of contacting a factory like she did for the fashion house, every minute was important.

The most important of it being the funds she required to source raw materials... There were a hundred things she needed and it was all sitting in that bank.

She dialed the number for the bank manager she had spoken to just two days ago.

Her heart hammered painfully, thudding faster and faster, an ominous pounding she couldn't breathe past. There could be only one man behind this. Her stomach twisted as the bank manager coughed on the other end of the phone. His answer was curt, immediate as though he had been rehearsing the explanation, waiting for Leah to call.

They couldn't use the trust fund as security to approve her loan because—Leah could hear the hushed reverence in the manager's voice as he uttered the name—the trustee overseeing her fund had denied the use of the trust fund, *her trust fund*, as security.

Stavros.

Leah threw the handset across the room, every inch of her shaking. She kicked the chair aside, the impact of it jarring up her leg, every nerve cell in her humming with outrage.

How much more was he going to punish her? How long was she going to let him?

She picked up the phone again, her vision blurry now with unchecked tears. Her throat burned as she took a deep breath, her thumb hovering over the numbers on the handset.

She wanted to demand an explanation, she wanted to...

But what was the point? His secretary would politely tell her that he was not available. It was the same answer she had received over the last year every time she had tried to contact him. Even though they both lived in Athens, they might as well have been living on the opposite ends of the planet.

She bit her lower lip, her nails digging into her skin. A sob built inside her chest, fury rising through her like a storm that could swallow her in its clutches.

She had to put an end to this. She had to break free of the leash he bound her with, controlling her every step, every choice, while he enjoyed his life. She had let him do it for five years.

Five years of a sterile life, five years of being his prisoner—that she had accepted out of guilt and fear.

Scrubbing the tears from her cheeks, she pulled up the society feature she had purposely clicked away from this morning on her laptop.

Stavros's business partner and her grandfather's second godson, Dmitri Karegas, was throwing a party aboard his yacht.

Stavros and Dmitri were cut from the same cloth—breathtakingly gorgeous, built their empires from nothing under her grandfather Giannis's guidance, and considered themselves gods, their will law for the normal mortals they walked amongst.

Stavros hated parties with an intensity Leah had never been able to understand, but Dmitri would be there.

She just had to make sure the decadent playboy, who apparently was always surrounded by a group of willing women, noticed her presence aboard his latest toy.

Had to, somehow, gain his attention.

Her stomach clenched as she shoved the bedroom door open and walked toward the closet.

Every step toward it, every thought in this direction—was like walking to her own doom.

But Stavros had left her no choice…left her with no way out.

She dialed another number on her phone and booked a taxi. A shiver traveled over her spine as she viciously pushed the cotton tops and skirts in her closet away until she reached the end.

She pulled the gold silk dress, the one designer label she had kept, her fingers shaking violently as she realized how little fabric there was of the dress. Her back would be totally bare, which meant she had to go without a bra.

And it would leave most of her legs, her thighs bare too. So no underwear either.

Five years ago, she hadn't even blinked when she had worn it. Had thought it nothing to parade around with Alex and Calista, showing every bit of skin she could expose, barely looking decent…

And she had been almost twenty pounds heavier…

Just thinking of how she must have looked then made her cringe.

What the hell had the designer been thinking? What the hell had she been thinking?

She had been trying to please Calista, who had decreed she wear it that night… That's what she had been thinking.

Yet nothing else in her closet would do for tonight.

Of all the things to think about when her life was eternally stuck in this rut, when the very walls of this apartment were closing in on her…

Her palms were sweating as she pulled the dress to herself. The dress would fall scandalously above her knees, just about covering her buttocks.

It was the most outrageous dress she owned, the sartorial equivalent of a tramp and she had worn it the night Stavros had decided her fate. Fitting then that it was the one that would at least get her an audience with the man who was her jailor.

Every muscle in her trembled, and her mouth was coated with bitter fear as she walked into the bathroom and splashed water on her face.

He was going to explode, he was going to despise her even more, if that was possible. But she couldn't bear this… this isolation anymore.

She couldn't bear to continue like this. Something had to give.

Leah clutched the leather seat of the taxi, holding onto it a like a lifeline, the curious glances the cabbie threw her way doing nothing to propel her out.

She took a deep breath and looked out the dirty window. The marina was busy, a few of the yachts moored there highlighted by the setting sun. But even amidst the loud luxury, one yacht stood out, its gleaming white exterior splendid in the setting sun's light.

She took the bills out of her gold-lined clutch and handed it over. *This was it.*

She didn't let herself think, she didn't let herself even

look around over the next few minutes. Keeping her shoulders straight, head held high, she reached the security personnel guarding the planked entrance. Except for the glimpse of recognition in his gaze, the six-footer didn't budge a muscle.

Leah raised a brow haughtily, the gesture taking everything she had.

Yes, she had spent the past five years working as an apprentice in a mid-level fashion house, away from the spotlight, locked up in a bubble where no one knew who she was, where no one cared except that she didn't put a toe out of line.

She slept, she woke up, went to work, went back to her apartment, ate dinner and fell into bed again, while Stavros's minion, Mrs. Kovlakis, her housekeeper, watched her, made sure she didn't comit any further scandalous acts. But that didn't mean anyone had forgotten what she had done, or what Stavros had done to her as punishment.

Especially in this crowd that hung on to every word from Stavros's lips as if it was the Holy Bible. It felt like an eternity but only a few seconds passed before the man stepped aside. Taking his proffered hand, Leah stepped onto the deck, her guts twisting into a gooey mess.

For a few dazzling minutes, she forgot why she was there as she ventured further. Uniformed waiters passed around champagne. The party was in full swing on the deck, inebriated, sweaty bodies pressing against each other...

Excitement and an electric energy touched the air, and she swayed automatically to the music.

So everything she had heard of Dmitri's parties was true...and strangely the antithesis of everything Stavros was. So he wouldn't be here. But she needed to be recognized, which meant she had to grab Dmitri's attention, especially if he was busy ravishing his latest arm candy.

Smiling for the first time since this afternoon, she

walked toward the glittering glass bar that she had read about, planted herself on one barstool, ordered a cosmo and proceeded to get drunk.

Stavros Sporades frowned as his cell phone beeped for the tenth time in the last five minutes. He picked up the phone and smiled at Helene, loath to ruin their private dinner. It was the first time he was relaxing in a month and he guarded his downtime as fiercely as he did his work time.

He picked up his champagne flute and took a sip before clicking Yes.

Dmitri's drawling tone reverberated in his ears. "She's here. Aboard my yacht."

Stavros fell back against the seat in silent shock. Only one woman being aboard Dmitri's yacht would cause him to call.

Leah.

His blood pumped furiously through his veins. "Are you sure it's her?"

A mocking laugh met his ears. "It took me a few minutes to recognize her, but yes, it's her. She's drunk and dancing."

Drunk and dancing...

Instead of seeing Leah's face, he saw his sister Calista, unmoving and pale in death. He had tried so hard to find some kind of closure from Calista's untimely death, and yet, the anger and the powerlessness were just as raw, just as fresh.

Gritting his jaw, Stavros calmly pocketed his phone. Fury reverberated within, leaving his chest perversely cold. He made his apologies to Helene and exited the rooftop restaurant.

She's doing very well, Mr. Sporades, Mrs. Kovlakis had said about Leah, in her nasal voice on his weekly phone call. *Almost a changed personality, if you can believe.*

Had the woman been just telling him what he had wanted to hear?

Within minutes, his pilot landed them on Dmitri's luxury yacht.

He stepped onto the helipad, a corrosive anger roped with heart-pounding fear running through him. "Where is she?"

His gaze deceptively calm, Dmitri pointed to the dance floor on the lower deck. "I could have had the security personnel grab her, but I think that would have made the situation worse."

Stavros nodded, unwilling to meet his oldest friend's eyes.

His control was barely teetering on the edge as it was. He didn't want to be thankful for the fact that it could have been worse, much worse than Dmitri's yacht.

He didn't want to feel grateful that it was just alcohol, not drugs.

Cristos, he didn't want to set eyes on the woman he had married as punishment and penance.

He didn't want to set eyes on Leah.

Even in the drunken haze caused by the three cosmos she had consumed, Leah knew the exact moment Stavros had reached the dimly lighted dance floor.

The hairs on her neck shot up, her stomach plummeted. An unbearable cold claimed her skin even though the breeze from the sea was warm. She shook her head slowly to clear the fog and looked up.

The famous, specially commissioned, glittering glass bar that was the prize of Dmitri's yacht showed a hundred reflections of Stavros. Narrowly sculpted face as if a sculptor had been asked to keep austerity at the front of his mind, the sharp, long bridge of his nose that was arrogance embodied, the cruel slash of his wide mouth that instantly reminded her of that one punishing kiss, and the tawny, long-lashed eyes...

And the hatred blazing in them when he met her gaze

in the glass—a hundred flickers of fire that could scorch her in so many ways.

Nausea bubbled through her and Leah stumbled.

Shaking uncontrollably, she wrapped her fingers around the nape of the twenty-something guy she had been dancing with for the last quarter of an hour. Although it was more him holding her boneless body up.

Thankfully, the stranger's face was blurry to her. She didn't want to remember anything from this night tomorrow. She moved her feet slowly in rhythm with the beat of hip-hop blaring around them. His hands moved over her hips, hesitated, then moved back up over her back, before embracing her.

Her stomach quivered, the faint whisper of something as mundane as comfort warming her insides.

How pathetic had her life become if the man's thin body comforted her?

Willing herself to ignore the cloud of black thunder she could sense around her, she dragged in a raspy breath. Softly ominous whispers emerged through the din and music, the sweaty, swaying bodies parting without his uttering a word. It was as if even the air in that lower deck was suspended in the face of the thundering storm.

She pulled herself up and kissed her companion's smooth, almost boyish jaw and whispered *sorry*.

It wasn't the poor guy's fault that he had no knowledge of who she was or he wouldn't have dared to touch her. Would have sidled away from her, treating her like a pariah as the rest of the crowd had done once Dmitri had walked by, his gray gaze devouring her with unhurried interest. Once they had all realized she was Leah Huntington Sporades, prisoner and possession of Stavros Sporades, not to be looked at or even spoken to, especially by another man.

Because, Alex, her one friend who hadn't turned away from her, who had tried to contact her even after Calista's death and her marriage, had ended up in jail on some trumped-up charges Stavros and that equally arrogant Dmitri had fabricated out of thin air.

The depth of her hatred for Stavros left her shaking uncontrollably.

A steel band wound around her waist and jerked her away from the stranger. Maybe he was even a teenager, she thought, feeling old and tired at just twenty-four.

She fell against a solid, hard frame with a soft thud that knocked the breath out of her.

Unlike the man she had been dancing with, Stavros was all hard, unforgiving muscle that sent her body into shock at the contact.

Long fingers held her arms in a grip this short of hurting and turned her, the heat emanating from his body hitting her like a wave of the sea.

Blinking, Leah raised her gaze and then shied away immediately.

Coward, a voice mocked her inside but she didn't care.

The soporific effect of the alcohol she had consumed stunting the hatred that buzzed her blood, she went like a doll incapable of independent motion as he picked her up and threw her over his shoulder.

The jutting bones of his shoulders dug into her rib cage, her breasts crushed by his muscular back but Leah refused to let even a whimper emerge.

The world tilted upside down and a tear seeped through despite her efforts. The quiet hush that preceded them was like the calm before the storm...

She had done what she had wanted to do.

She had made a spectacle of herself, she had Stavros's attention.

Except nothing could numb her to the blistering contempt that had flashed in his gaze in the split second she had looked into it.

She squeezed her eyes shut and gave herself over to the haze in her head.

* * *

Leah jerked and breathed in great gulps as ice-cold water drenched her from all sides. She yelped and scooted back on her bum but there was no escape from the chilly spray. Her breath came in quick, short bursts, her lungs struggling to pump it out.

Another hard surface at her back thwarted her attempt at escape and she gave up, shuddering.

Reaching out with her hands, she touched cold marble. Her gaze flew open and she blinked to get the water out. The gold silk plastered to her body offered no protection against the cold. Shivering, she looked around, the chill sinking into her blood, raising goose bumps over her skin.

With shaking hands, she pushed her wet hair out of her face, her mascara running in black rivers down her fingers. So much for waterproof.

Blew out a long breath through her mouth and tried to make sense of her bearings.

She didn't need to turn to see Stavros standing there, watching her with malicious satisfaction. Could muster not a bit of surprise at what he had done.

Even through every nerve in her flinched at the cold, Leah could still feel his wrath, the heat of his anger. She stretched her arm, still shaking and turned off the glinting silver faucets.

Suddenly, all she wanted to do was curl up in the marble tub and close her eyes. Her body sank into the tub as if her muscles had no rigidness anymore.

"Get out of the tub." The quiet command landed on her like a slap, jerking her back to the purgatory that waited for her.

And the man who wanted to punish her for the rest of her life.

Even after years, she had no strength to face Stavros, couldn't face...

No, she wouldn't feel sorry for herself. Not after all that she had done today to just see him.

Clutching the marble, she pulled herself up to her legs.

Seconds piled on as the shaking in her legs subsided and the luxuriously spacious bathroom stopped swaying in front of her.

Blinking at the glare of light from a crystal chandelier overhead, she took in the dark oak floors and the blue sea outside the window.

Instead of the din, so nerve-racking that she swayed, utter calm reigned.

On shaking legs, she stepped out, dripping water everywhere. Her shoulders shook with the effort it took to keep standing.

A towel came straight at her with a resounding, "Cover yourself."

She buried her face in the plush cotton, taking the few seconds of privacy it afforded to shore up her defenses. But the contemptuous note in his tone pricked, as if a needle had punctured her skin and drew blood.

Fighting the urge to stay behind the towel, she straightened her spine and threw the towel back. "I'm wearing a dress, thank you. It's your fault if it reveals more than it covers," she said, brazening it out.

The plush cotton landed on one arrogant shoulder and she saw those broad shoulders tense. Felt his perusal as if he had laid those big hands on her...

Which was the strangest, scariest thought she had to have ever had.

"I see that you still don't know what is good for you then, Leah."

Gathering her wet hair in one hand, she squeezed the water out. Forced an indifference she didn't feel in the least. Because the reality of her reaction to him was too scary. "More like an allergic reaction to you. I'd rather catch pneumonia and die than be saved by you."

He reached her suddenly, a wall of fury and contempt that narrowed her very world to him.

Fear and confusion and so many things that she had battled over the last decade deluged her.

The overhead monster lighting illuminated his stark features—a sharper slap to her senses than the ice-cold water, but it was the tawny eyes that knocked the breath out of her.

Calista.

Calista had had those same eyes, except they had been kind, quick to smile, always in search of the next thrill, luring men into her orbit like a spider did with her web.

Her gut twisted into that insidious, painful knot that crept into her when she didn't make a conscious effort to turn her mind to something else, something other than Calista and that night.

It didn't help. Nothing did. But amidst the shock of seeing him again, something else penetrated through with an insidious clarity as he neared her.

Set against the severity of his face, the lush lashes and the glittering eyes stood out like an oasis in a desert. Rendering the man impossibly gorgeous, darkly stunning.

His scent was alien, yet alluring.

Leah breathed in a lungful before she could stop, a feverish shiver taking hold of her limbs that had nothing to do with her wet dress.

"Stavros, I—"

Long fingers crawled up her nape into her scalp, tilted her up, while the other hand clasped her jaw loosely.

He studied her every feature with such thorough appraisal that her insides turned into gooey pulp.

No one had even touched her in so long…it had to be why she could feel his touch like a brand on her skin… why such heat was pooling under her skin and rushing to the fore.

Why she wanted to sink into his rough touch more than she wanted to breathe…

Until she realized what he was doing.

He was checking if her pupils were dilated, wondering if she was high.

She stared into his glittering gaze, noted the concrete set of his jaw. Saw a shadow of something in his face that hurled the words past her throat. "I'm not high, Stavros." It came out as a whisper, an entreaty, and Leah recoiled at that pleading tone.

When he didn't relent, she grabbed his wrists. Every cell in her rose to attention as the whorls of hair there tickled her palm, as a shot of electricity sparked in the air.

"I remember the last time you said those words…" He sounded as if he was far away, in another place, another time.

Leah jerked his hand away, the heat from his body potent in its draw. Her skin tingled, every muscle in her rearing to get closer to him to soak up that deceptive warmth. She would freeze to death before she sought anything from him. "I'm telling the truth, Stavros."

I have never touched drugs, she wanted to scream, like she had the night when Calista had died. But he hadn't even acknowledged her teary words.

His teeth bared in an entirely cold smile. "Ditching your security detail, lying to Mrs. Kovlakis, appearing on Dmitri's yacht of all places—which is infamous for its wild parties, and knocking back drinks, forgive me if I don't take your word for it."

How unfailingly polite he was… He had done that before too, even as he had ruined her life.

You can either marry me or you can go to jail, Leah. The choice is yours.

"It got your attention, didn't it?" she said, realizing too late she had given herself away. Not that she had meant to keep it a secret.

CHAPTER TWO

"WHAT?"

Stavros loosened his grip on Leah, struggling to get himself under control, struggling to get his neurons to fire again.

Guilt roiled through him, a heavy pulsing weight in his gut, something he had managed to subdue into a dull ache. But one look at Leah was enough to unman him again.

He took a step back as a sharp scent combined with the scent of her skin teased him softly, the cold from her arms clinging to his fingertips.

Frowning, he muttered a curse.

For the first time in his adult life, he lost the razor-sharp concentration that had made him a force to be reckoned with in the business circles of Athens. For several seconds.

"What did you say?"

She glared at him. "You, Stavros. You were the prize in this tacky show. If you had returned a single phone call, if you had read even one of my numerous emails to you... So, of course, I had to lower myself to your standards, didn't I?"

"My standards?" He was beginning to sound like an idiot and yet, it seemed his brain's higher functions had fractured.

An ominous thud started somewhere in the regions of his heart. His gaze swept over her with a swift greed he had no chance of curbing. The gold silk dress was almost the color of her skin that had a golden tone that no amount of spray tan could manufacture.

The result was that the dress moved sinuously against those high breasts, dipped at her waist, painting an erotic picture of almost nudity that had knocked him for sixes when he had first spied her at the bar.

Any traces of the curvy, awkwardly brazen girl he had married were gone. Instead, the woman who stood there—the delicate contours of her face rendering her infinitely fragile, her body bordering on scrawny, which made her breasts stand out even more—was a complete stranger.

"This is what you expect of me, isn't it? So I delivered. And here you are, in front of me, for the first time in five years as if I had conjured you with a spell."

A spell, as preposterous as it sounded, could be the only thing that could explain how dumbfounded he was.

Her long brown hair was plastered to her scalp and sprayed her face with drops of water when she rubbed it roughly. And every move was touched with an elegant sensuality that, he knew, was more innate than manufactured.

He had handled her so roughly just now, blinded by fury and fear. And any time he felt that unbalanced, his temper took a nasty dive, as his sister used to call it. "You look like… What the hell have you done to yourself?" he said, his control snapping.

She didn't even flinch, although he saw her lashes flicker down for a second. Her oval face was so thin and fine-boned that her light brown eyes were like dark, murky pools in it. Her arms were thin, too, but at least there was muscle tone to it.

Her hand curving over her hip, her tarty dress clinging to her wet skin, her teeth chattering in her mouth, she thrust one bony hip out in a seductive little moment. "What? You don't like my utterly fabulous and thin body? Your prison sentence has had at least one perk, Stavros. I lost so much weight that even the models parading through the fashion house keep asking me for tips. I can't count the number of times Marco has asked me to do a shoot, told me I would be a natural…"

It was the utterly uncaring, blind privilege in her words that broke the haze from Stavros's eyes. She was manipulating him, working herself under his skin like she always did, and yet he could do nothing to stop her.

From the moment he had laid eyes on her, Leah had been nothing but a spoilt, selfish, pleasure-seeking brat who didn't know the value of what she had or the people she hurt around her.

So she looked different. It didn't mean anything except that she had another bow in her arsenal for causing trouble. The first thing he needed to do was to get that… body covered up.

He grabbed her wrist, realized how fragile she was, and loosened his grip. Dragged her with him to Dmitri's bedroom.

"Wow." Her unconcerned exclamation boiled his blood anew.

He stilled on the way to the wardrobe, her stretched out body on Dmitri's vast bed sending the most insane urge to pull her off it.

Cristos, something was wrong with him.

For several seconds, he stared blindly at the rows of neatly arranged Savile Row shirts. Wondered what he was doing in there.

"Dmitri does know how to party and live in style, doesn't he?"

With a curse, he grabbed a shirt and threw it at her just as she pulled herself up. Her legs, long and toned, with black leather strips from her three-inch sandals winding round and round to her calves, glimmered against the dark red of Dmitri's sheets.

"Let me get this straight. You dressed like a ten-pound hooker, got drunk and plastered yourself over that boy to get my attention? And it has nothing to do with the fact that a normal, alcohol- and drug-free life was getting to you?"

The shirt he threw came flying back at him, missing him narrowly. He turned and stilled.

The goose bumps on her skin stood out, her eyes huge in her oval face.

"I've been trying to get in touch with you for a year. If you had the decency to speak to me, I wouldn't have had to do anything so drastic. It's the first time I've touched alcohol in five years. Not surprisingly, I'm not driven to drink anymore."

For all his self-discipline over the last few years, he couldn't stop looking. He couldn't stop devouring every small bit about her like he couldn't stop breathing.

Her nipples pebbled against the flimsy dress, her breasts, unsupported by a bra, heaving with her harsh breathing.

She looked like a red-blooded man's wet dream, and he was in no way impervious to the effect.

No!

This was Leah, a chain of duty and reminder of his failure around his neck. He had absolutely no interest in her except to keep her safe.

With ruthless will that had directed that he marry the woman responsible for his sister's death, he cut that line of thought.

"Meaning I drove you to drink?" When she remained resolutely mute, he took another clearing breath. He couldn't get this riled up over her. "Good for you. But I'm sure some habits are harder to kick than others. Like finding a scapegoat to hide your weaknesses behind."

She flinched. He saw her swallow and turn away.

Hated the vicious satisfaction her pale face gave him. This was why he had avoided seeing her for so long.

With her mere presence, Leah reduced him to a hurtful, raging bastard with no control, ripped off any semblance of closure he deluded himself into achieving.

"I didn't make a spectacle to discuss my shortcomings with you." Said in that flippant voice that he had heard so many times.

But her whole body shook with the breath she dragged in. Curved like a bow, her pink mouth looked inviting. Like it was made for mindless kissing.

He studied it with rising fascination, the relentless drag of guilt and anger he felt in her presence dulled by something new, something far more dangerous.

He pushed a hand through his hair, wondering what was getting into him. "You have my attention now, Leah. Tell me, what is that you want?"

"You've proved to the whole world what an honorable man you are by marrying the disreputable Katrakis heiress. You've kept your word to Giannis. You've punished me for five years for my sins and more. Now…please, cut the leash on my life, Stavros."

Her gaze held steady when he looked up, the fluttering pulse at her neck the only sign of her desperation. She linked her hands in front of her, and for a moment, Stavros couldn't help but be impressed by her determination to keep a lid on her temper.

It was like watching a volcano trying to contain the lava within.

"Did you think for a second what you did would completely defeat your goal, Leah? How could finding you drunk and plastered over someone persuade me to let you go? Within the month, you will be back to it all, the drugs, the parties. And I can't let that happen."

Every drop of blood fled from her face. "You cut me off from the entire world. You cut me off from my friends. You have your goons watch over me night and day. You… And that's fine too.

"But…you've been ignoring my emails, your hateful secretary is forever deflecting me. You…you can't just

take me on as a responsibility and then…just lock me up.
I'm not a possession to safeguard. You left me no choice."

"There are always choices. It's a pity that with everything you have in the world, you never learned to make
the right ones."

"I'm not interested in discussing the past or the present." If she did, she would crumple to the floor in a helpless
heap. Like she had been for the first couple of months after
Calista had died. "All I care about is myself and my future."

"Of course." His jaw tightened. "So you have nothing
to say to me, nothing to ask?"

She shook her head. "I have a hundred things to orga-
nize for my collection. I'm already behind. All I want is a
phone call authorizing the release of the…"

He prowled toward her in a slow gait that sent her heart
thumping like a bass drum.

"You haven't seen me, or anyone for five years. Aren't
you even remotely curious, Leah?"

"About what?" she managed to whisper, under the thrall
of his mesmerizing gaze.

With a smooth flick of his wrist, he tugged her and she
fell into him with a gasp. Every muscle in her body sighed
at the contact with his hard one. A little more pressure
and he had her locked in his arms with their faces only
inches apart. Leaving her with no choice except to look
into the anger that turned his eyes into dark gold. "About
how your grandfather is doing, you ungrateful little brat."
At her gasp, his hold tightened further, this short of hurting. Sinuous heat burst in her belly and Leah struggled.
"Is it too much to hope you would care about the man who
took care of you when your father died?"

With a grunt, Leah pushed him back, hating the fact
that he had muddled with her head with so little effort. She
couldn't let on how rattled she was by his presence, how out
of balance she felt when he touched her, even innocently.

She breathed in roughly, gritting her jaw so tight that

she would need to see a dentist soon. There should have been smoke coming out of her ears too. "First of all…I'm not sixteen anymore so stop calling me a brat.

"Secondly, not that I have to explain myself to you, I know how Giannis is doing. I speak to his nurse every day."

She instantly regretted her words when she saw the disbelief in his gaze.

Turning away from him, she walked to the mini fridge in the corner, needing the time away from his scrutiny to compose herself. Grabbed a bottle and gulped the water down so fast that her throat burned at the chill.

And yet she could feel the heat pooling under her skin as he watched her from the other side of the room, could feel an unnamed charge building up in the room…

This slicing awareness of him, this reaction to his nearness…it was intolerable and utterly frightening. Stavros had only wreaked destruction on her life—why didn't her body understand that?

"You haven't visited him once in five years."

Her chest ached at the thought of seeing Giannis. God, how she wanted to see that kind smile… Even through his heart attack and triple bypass surgery five years ago, Giannis had survived. She wouldn't risk it by seeing him now.

"My relationship with Giannis is none of your business."

His mouth stretched into a smile, the straight upper lip losing its severity in the process. "I'm making it mine."

"And I'm saying 'No more.' I have spent five years living a life you dictated, Stavros, down to the food I ate, the clothes I wore, the people I spoke to. Whatever you think needed fixing in me, it is fixed now. I want to lead my life, I want to build a career…" Frustration filled her throat with tears. "What more do you need to be convinced that I can lead my own life?"

"Not getting a phone call from Dmitri that you are

drunk and plastered over some boy would have been a start."

"I told you why I did that. If I hadn't, you would have gone another decade without answering my phone calls." She hated that her every action was being driven by him. That even in her own mind, she had no freedom. And it could not continue.

"I have spoken to a friend of mine. Philip is a lawyer." She stepped back from him, willing herself to stay strong. "I'm aware of my rights, Stavros. There are a hundred different reasons that could be cited and accepted by the court for a divorce."

"A divorce?"

"Yes. I want a divorce. I want to never see you again. And I'm sure the thought of being rid of me forever fills you with happiness. So give us both what we want."

A small smile touched his mouth but didn't reach that compelling gaze. Again, Leah had a feeling that it hid so much she didn't know. "You have rights and lawyers. But it could take years if I didn't agree, Leah. We could be celebrating a ten-year anniversary before we even get through the preliminaries."

"Is this what I have become for you?" Leah grabbed the edge of the desk to hide the trembling of her hands, a scream building away in her chest.

Hot tears prickled behind her eyelids. "Someone to punch, something to punish eternally so that you can feel better about what happened to Calista? Believe me, I wish it had been me that ended up dead that night and not her. But you know what? Wishing doesn't make anything come true."

Because even though she had never touched drugs in her life, she had enabled Calista that night. And that guilt choked her.

For the first time that evening, or maybe in forever, he

looked so shocked that Leah would have celebrated it as a victory if not for the gnawing in her gut.

Slowly, he recovered, those long lashes hiding his expression. "I have never wished that you had died instead that night, Leah."

She didn't want to believe him. But Stavros was never less than honest.

Of course he wouldn't have wished Giannis Katrakis's granddaughter's death. His control, not only over his actions, but even his very thoughts had always disconcerted and fascinated her in equal measure.

He lived by such a stringent code of his own rules, and applied it to everyone around him that no one could really hold up to it.

Not Dmitri, not Calista and definitely not her.

Recovering from the memory, she shook her head. "Right. You didn't wish my death because who else will you take out your sadistic side on if I were gone?"

"You call the last decade of your presence in my life sadism. I call it masochism."

She knew, *had always known*, what he thought of her. But hearing it in his own words… Her fingers pressed into the glass in her hand, the urge to throw the glass, water and all, at his head bubbling up inside her.

His amused gaze followed her shaky movements. "Try it."

The utter satisfaction in his voice got through to her like nothing else could.

He expected this of her. He expected a juvenile tantrum and she had already catered to him today and for years. Every time he had warned her to not do something, she had done that and more. Had lashed out against him from the moment she had landed in Greece.

Hating Stavros, especially when he had continuously given her ample reasons, had been easier than dealing with the grief and fear inside her.

No more, Leah.

There was power in that choice, power in saying she wouldn't give him the satisfaction of being right about her anymore.

Instead, she took a deep breath, reminded herself why she was here. It would be great if Stavros released those funds to her. But she had known it wouldn't be that simple.

Any other man would have sent the woman he thought responsible for his sister's death to the other end of the world.

Instead, hours after he had buried Calista, he had bound her to him in the most sacred of bonds.

She didn't even care about the divorce. The mockery of her marriage had never meant anything to her. All she wanted was to succeed, to give her life meaning, to take the joy she had always found in designing and creating to the next step.

"What do I have to do that you will release those funds?"

"Will you do anything I ask of you?"

Something in the silky tone of his voice—a flicker of interest maybe, nudged her into panic zone again. "My personal life is my own. Even with the shackles you bound me with, I have friends who mean something to me. If you order me to cut ties with them, I won't.

"Last time you cut off my friends from me and gained control over my life, I was…I was too…"

"Too high to even notice what was going on around you?"

She hadn't even gone on the anti-anxiety medication that had been prescribed after her dad's death, hadn't wanted to numb the grief of his death.

But it was pointless to defend herself when he had already passed judgment.

"I know how much you resented my responsibility from the moment I stepped off that plane. It doesn't have to be like that anymore."

Walking around the desk, he reached her side, and Leah fought the automatic impulse to step back, to keep some distance between them.

With his Greek-god good looks and smoldering arrogance, Stavros had always made her feel like the proverbial ugly duckling, made her feel even more awkward than she already had, surrounded by her grandfather's high-class society friends.

It seemed like a thoroughly unwelcome awareness took the place of her anxiety now. The faint stubble on his tight cheeks, the perfectly etched curve of his mouth…

The collar of his dress shirt was open, showing his olive skin. Holding her breath in, she pulled her gaze to his.

Every nerve in her body thrummed as he neared her. At thirty-three, he was a decade older than her. So why couldn't he have grown a paunch and become bald? Couldn't fate or whatever it was up above give her a break at least in this?

Couldn't he have been a little less gorgeous?

"If you have waited five years, what's three more months for a divorce? Or is this Philip more than just a lawyer?"

"Philip is only a friend. And if you want to continue satisfying your twisted sense of duty…fine."

Stavros watched in rising fascination as she closed her eyes and pulled in a long breath.

Shame filled him as he took in her slender frame. He hadn't seen her once in five years. He hadn't even made a call. Had just left her to Mrs. Kovlakis's care.

It had been unbearable to even look at her after Calista's death.

Theos, he had been so angry with her…

He had granted her request to apprentice at the fashion house, and yet, he hadn't really done his duty, had he? Marrying her to protect her from fortune hunters that had always surrounded her like vultures, to protect her from her own reckless lifestyle, as he had promised Giannis, had only been the first step.

He had let grief and anger distract him. It had been easy to forget about her, easier even to tolerate her presence in his life from a distance.

A possession to safeguard?

She was right—it had gone on too long. He had resented his future with her for long enough.

"I've learned all I could at the fashion house. I have made some good contacts, and I would like to leave it now."

Tension swathed him as she interrupted his thoughts. He should never have left her alone for so long, shouldn't have given her this chance to go on the offensive.

"Leave and go where?"

"Ideally, I would love to go to New York City. But it—"

"New York and your inheritance—I can see where this is going."

"—will be like starting all over," she continued, glaring at him. "I have made some good contacts here—buyers at retail stores, models who like what I have come up with so far. So I decided against it. But I do need to take the next step now. The fashion industry moves so fast that waiting until the few people that like my designs forget me will harm any future I have in it."

"What is the next step?"

Sudden energy filled her eyes. "I'm going to take a chance and start freelancing, do custom orders for now. Right now, I have interest from a woman who buys for a small retail store in London."

"Going out on your own, especially in your field, is a risky venture. Shouldn't you continue at the fashion house?"

"I have been making clothes all my life, Stavros. I have worked there for seven years and except for being allowed to give input on a senior designer's creations, I don't have any growth there."

"But you don't know anything about running a business."

"You grew up on some itty-bitty farm and Dmitri... what was he...a drug runner or a pimp? I forget... The point is both of you knew less than squat when Giannis brought you here."

He continued staring at her, his silence wreaking havoc on her breathing.

"I need to take this shot. And I need money up front for all the costs. I can't access my trust fund unless you stop controlling it, unless you step down from your role as..."

"Ahhh..." He smirked and Leah wished she could get away with slapping the hateful man. But one wrong breath now and he would never listen to her again.

"That's what this is all about. Money."

"Yes, money," she added, mimicking his sarcastic tone. Easy for him to look down upon her when he had gazillions of it. "Money that my father left me and has nothing to do with you or Giannis or my mother or the bloody Katrakis dynasty's inheritance."

"Fine."

Was that it? So easy? Leah let out a long breath. Excitement fizzed through her. She would call her contact at the textile factory as soon as she got out. She would have to finalize and place orders for the raw materials, would have to hire someone to help with the sewing, would have to order equipment...

"Show me a proposal for this alleged business you want to start. If I find it sound," he said, stressing how improbable he found the very idea, "I will invest in it myself."

Anger and hurt ripped through Leah, leaving her trembling all over. Her chest was so tight that it was a miracle she could breathe.

She wanted to smash the expensive porcelain vase on the side table next to her, she wanted to let the scream building away in her chest loose, she wanted to...

"I don't want your investment. I don't want anything from you. I want my money. I want this...my career—I need this to be about me, Stavros, something I love doing, something I can take on without fear. Something I give all of myself to."

"I should have made my intentions clearer to you far sooner. You were right, I shouldn't have let it go on for so long. But now that you are here, I will correct the situation immediately."

Her heart lurched into her throat, cutting off Leah's breath. Whatever it was that he meant, it wasn't going to be remotely what she wanted. "What do you mean?"

"When I gave my word to Giannis that I would protect you, even from yourself, I didn't mean it temporarily, Leah. I meant the *until death do us* part. Whatever way that death might come for you. So let's get two things straight."

He looked like someone had carved his features in stone, removed every ounce of emotion from it. "This lawyer friend of yours… he should know better than to tangle with my wife.

"Secondly, you'll move in with me."

"What? Why?"

"Because it's high time we started our life together.

"And as for your career, we will get a fashion house, London or Milan or Paris, whatever you choose, to launch a line for you. As my wife, you will lack for nothing."

CHAPTER THREE

LAUNCH A LINE from a top design house in the world? Lack for nothing as his wife?

His wife?

He had to be joking; he had always liked making her miserable!

You cannot see that boy anymore, Leah...

No more trips to New York...

Giannis allows you far too much financial freedom but not anymore...

Leah met his gaze and everything within her stilled.

Stavros Sporades didn't give his word or make a promise easily. When he did...

Fear struck her so hard that her knees shuddered under her.

He instantly moved forward to catch her but Leah jerked away from him. "Don't come near me," she whispered.

She grabbed the door to stop from sliding to the floor in a puddle. She wanted to scream her denial but what left her mouth was a soft gasp.

He would never forgive her, or himself, for Calista's death, never even give her a chance. Would punish them both for the rest of their lives.

And to even contemplate being his wife in the true sense of the word...

Perversely, she felt a chilly calm inside instead of a boiling rage. "When I decided to come here today, I didn't even care about whether I was married to you or not. I didn't care about being so lonely all these years…friends I knew once living their life to the fullest… I lived it as if I deserved to be punished. But now…I won't quietly accept your word this time.

"I'm going to file for divorce, Stavros."

A tic played in his jaw, the only thing that betrayed his even gaze. He looked insurmountable, like a boulder intent on crushing her. "Lawyers and court proceedings cost money."

That patronizing tone set her teeth on edge. "I will sell myself if I have to, to pay for it. Within the week, I will move out of that flat, will be handing in my resignation at the fashion house. The moment I step out of here, I'm going to call Philip and tell him what I plan to do."

He moved to block her path, his gait predatory. "I'm not your enemy, Leah."

Panic pushed a hundred different flight routes in her head, one more desperate than the next. "No? Because God help me the day you decide that you are. If your goons even lay a finger on me, I will go to the media and start talking about how you have treated me over the last five years. I'll tell them I've been nothing but a glorified prisoner.

"I'm sure they would love to hear that saintly Stavros Sporades is nothing but a sadist."

"I do not care what the media calls me."

Nausea pooled in her mouth. "They will, of course, dig through the whole story again about that night and Calista."

If there was fury before in his eyes, now there was nothing but the bitterest loathing for her. And seeing as she felt the same inside, that she despised herself for how far she was taking this, his loathing couldn't touch Leah.

For once, his opinion of her couldn't hurt her, as twisted as it was.

"If he even hears a whiff of it—" a vein throbbed in his temple and his hands fisted at his side "—Giannis, who…

has done nothing but love you, he will be destroyed to see the Katrakis name dragged through mud. You will kill him with your stupid stunt, and my grandparents...they can't bear to think of Calista's death anymore."

"But you already know that I don't care about anyone but myself, don't you?" she bluffed, swallowing the bile that rose through her.

She couldn't betray the depth of pain that she held at bay every day thinking of her grandfather, of knowing he was close by but not seeing him.

Guilt ate through her insides. But she had no recourse except to threaten Stavros like this. She forced a smile, her cheeks hurting at her continued pretense. "If you don't want me to drag the Sporades name and the Katrakis name through mud, you will have to agree."

She opened the door and looked at him again, feeling truly afraid for the first time. She had gambled on the one person that she loved with all her heart. She could never hurt her grandfather. Even speaking about it like this was cutting her in two. But she had to make sure Stavros would believe her capable of it. "You will have to release those funds and you have to cut the strings you hold over my life. The choice is yours, Stavros."

"I thought I knew the depths of selfishness you could sink to, but you always manage to surprise me, Leah."

Desolation filled her at the utter resignation in his voice. That he believed her bluff didn't fill her with relief or gratitude however. Only painted a picture of what her life would be like with him.

And thinking of being caught in a circle of hatred and hero worship, she didn't have to try to sound like she didn't care. "What's new about that, Stavros? And who knows? Once I'm out of your life, you might even thank me for it."

Without stopping for even a breath, she rushed out of the bedroom and through the corridors, her legs barely holding her up.

She made it to the main deck before she collapsed onto the floor and clutched her knees. Leaning her head against her knees, she fought to corral her uneven breathing.

The very real possibility of Stavros still not believing what she had threatened sent a shaft of fear through her.

Her nape prickled as she heard someone approach, and instantly, she straightened her shoulders. She couldn't afford to let him see her like this… He would know that she had been bluffing. And she would be worse off than she had started today.

Breathing hard, she composed herself and looked up.

His hip lolling against the bar counter in casual elegance, Dmitri watched her with gray eyes. "Hello, Leah."

Shuddering, Leah swallowed the hard knot in her throat. She couldn't break down now, not when Stavros was so close.

A daring mockery in his gaze, Dmitri extended a hand to pull her up.

Leah grabbed his hand and pushed herself to her feet.

His hands were callous but didn't leave her shaking like Stavros's grip had done. His mocking gaze didn't compel her to react nor did his arrogant perusal leave her off balance and breathless. She didn't feel compelled to be better than she was, or to give up in frustration because nothing would ever change, as she did with Stavros.

She didn't feel anything except questionable warmth at seeing a familiar face.

Why Stavros of all men? Was she that much of a sucker for pain?

"I can see that you're—" Dmitri's gaze swept over her "—looking astonishingly well, so I'm not going to ask how you have been."

Set against Stavros's lacerating contempt, there was a slumbering, almost comforting quality to Dmitri that had always put her at ease. Looking into the bottomless depths of Dmitri's eyes now, she wondered how much of that warmth was a deceptive facade.

"Come, I'll take you home. Stavros will thank me for stopping *his precious wife* from getting arrested for indecent exposure."

Leah shivered, only barely stopping herself from covering her chest with her arms. Hearing herself referred to as Stavros's wife, even the mention of that bond that tied them together made her queasy inside, and Dmitri knew it.

Straightening her shoulders and resolutely holding her arms down, she glared at him. "Then he shouldn't have dumped me in that monstrous tub of yours."

His laughter swathed her. Leah ducked, just enough when he threw an arm to pull her to him.

"I'm not playing your games, Dmitri, so back off."

His eyes warmed up even more. The few times she had come into contact with him, he had at least had a kind smile for her, whether real or fake.

Familiar trust awoke in her, something inside her desperate for a friend after Stavros's stinging scorn.

Unless it was part of his game to get her to trust him and pump her for information so that he could take it back to Stavros... She sighed, feeling immensely tired and lonely.

"I have missed your sharp tongue all these years."

"Wish I could say the same, but I don't have your gift or charm for lying."

Reaching her, he hooked her arm through his and herded her toward the steps. "Let's not pretend about your talents. At least not with me."

Swallowing her fear, Leah dragged her feet. Dmitri saw far more than he let on. As different as they were, his friendship with Stavros was as inviolate as their devotion toward Giannis.

Donning that mask of reckless ignorance, Leah faced him. "I have no idea what you're talking about but I can find my own way, thank you."

"I heard your conversation, Leah."

"Then you're as uncivilized as they say."

He stared at her with unblinking eyes. "I had the yacht empty in five minutes but I couldn't leave. I was afraid of what you both would do to each other," he drawled silkily.

Every time she had seen Giannis with either Dmitri or Stavros, she had felt a yawning chasm in her chest knowing she could never share something like that with her own grandfather. And that it was her choice.

"It doesn't concern you, Dmitri."

Grabbing her arm, he turned her. "You're playing a dangerous game with Giannis's life, Leah. This is not like one of those antics you used to take up just to make Stavros furious."

That he had always seen through her ploys unnerved Leah. "All I want is my freedom, Dmitri, a chance to live my life. You get that, don't you?" she threw back at him, remembering bits and pieces of what Calista had told her about Dmitri's life before Giannis had plucked him off the streets of London.

"Try a different way then. For once, try to change the dynamic between you two, Leah."

"How?" she whispered, her voice breaking. "He's left me no choice. In that moment—" she pointed to the ominously quiet lower deck, her heart pounding in her chest "—it started as a bluff. But I... I don't know what I'm capable of anymore."

"Stavros and you are intent on destroying each other."

"Me destroy Stavros? All the power, all the cards are in his hands, Dmitri. As always." And the worst part was that she had given it all to him with her irresponsible behavior.

All she had today was the wretched power to hurt Giannis. And Leah was terrified that she would use that power. Desperation turned her words into a pitiful entreaty.

"If you count Stavros as your friend, if you really care

about Giannis's well-being, then convince Stavros that I don't need his brand of protection anymore. Please, Dmitri."

Two days later, Stavros and Dmitri were sparring in the ring in the ultra-sophisticated, custom-built gym attached to Dmitri's Athens apartment.

It had started when Stavros had suggested Dmitri could work his way out of a temper instead of losing it when Giannis had brought him to Athens years ago, morphed into a way for them to resolve arguments when they struggled to keep up with the rigorous, grueling schedule that Giannis set for them.

A habit they had carried into adulthood.

But today, Stavros was the one who felt bloodthirsty, like he was coming apart at the seams.

After two days in which he had been supremely unproductive, he still hadn't been able to master his reaction to seeing Leah.

You already know that I don't care about anyone but myself, don't you?

Her words rang through him, her glittering gaze and her vibrating body etched into his brain.

The brazen curve of her mouth, the reckless shrug with one hand on a bony hip, her dark brown hair drying in curls around that angelic face... *Cristo*, he still couldn't believe that...*boldly stunning* creature had been Leah.

Leah, who had jumped like a live wire when he had touched her without meaning to...

Leah, who, even at a naive sixteen, had somehow always pushed all the wrong buttons in him...

Leah, who was, even now, insidiously unfurling the iron fist with which he ruled his...

No!

Moving his right foot forward, Stavros swung his left hook with a vicious fury. The thwack of his knuckle against

Dmitri's jaw, and the hiss of his exhale, followed by the filthiest curse words reverberated in the quiet.

Shock flashed in Dmitri's eyes.

That Stavros had gone on the offense when it had always been about letting Dmitri work through one of his tempers, who learned to use his fists on the streets of London amidst gangs, spoke to his ragged control.

"Ding, ding," Dmitri mocked, dark amusement in his gaze. "Point for *Leah Huntington Sporades*."

Gritting his jaw, Stavros shot him a filthy look.

Massaging his jaw with one hand, Dmitri reached for a bottle of water with the other. "In all the years that we have known each other, you have never gone on the offensive. Today's win has to go to her."

Knowing how cunningly perceptive Dmitri was, Stavros decided to leave. It had been a miracle in itself that Dmitri had—showing what Giannis would have called uncharacteristic wisdom—left Stavros alone after Leah's latest stunt.

He didn't want to discuss Leah, with him of all people.

Dmitri's jaw was already black and blue, and for once, Stavros enjoyed the result of his loss of control. "Put some ice on it."

Dmitri stopped him with a hand on his arm. "You're pushing it too far, Stavros."

"Leave it alone, Dmitri." He knew exactly what his friend was talking about.

Moving around him, Dmitri blocked his path. "You went above and beyond what Giannis asked of you. Wash your hands off."

Giannis, to whom he and Dmitri owed their entire world, had asked for only one thing in return after becoming their salvation when they had been nothing but uneducated thugs.

And Stavros had failed spectacularly at it. "Have you forgiven yourself for everything you have ever done? Or failed to do?"

All emotion seeped out of Dmitri's face, leaving an uncaring mask in its place. "Do I look like I have been punishing myself for the last decade?"

Stavros made a doubtful sound of assent in his throat. "See you next week."

"Giannis asked you to protect her, Stavros, *ne*?" His breath hung in his throat as Stavros waited. "But what I saw two days ago… He should have entrusted me with Leah. I would have seduced her within the day, made her fall in love with me and then cast her aside after a week. She would have learned her lesson.

"But you—"

Stavros curled his hand around his friend's throat, fury filling every vein. The thought of Dmitri seducing and throwing away Leah made him crazy like a rabid dog he had once put down as a teenager. "She is not one of your party bunnies, Dmitri. She's…she's Leah."

His breathing loud to his own ears, Stavros stilled. Dmitri watched him with hooded eyes, not even trying to shake off his grip. They both knew what he had been about to say.

She is my wife.

When had he become so possessive of Leah? When had she gone from a chain around his neck to something that could incite him like this?

"To see Stavros Sporades's ironclad control unravel like this… But even a man made of stone would have noticed that gorgeous body. Leah could always get under your skin so easily," Dmitri continued, frowning, "but now, she has another weapon to wield against you."

"*Enough, Dmitri!* I don't interfere in your life nor pass judgment on it."

"But Leah is not just any woman. If you're doing this just because you suddenly have the hots for your little wife—"

"Some days, I don't know whether to call you friend or foe."

Dmitri didn't even blink. "You are the most honorable man I know, Stavros. Until I met you, I didn't know what it was. There are days when I still don't. But Leah's threat concerns Giannis. You need to make a decision soon."

"I already made one. Five years ago."

"Then why have you left her under someone else's care, kept her at a distance? Either she's truly your wife or you're through with her.

"You can't hang both your lives in limbo as if it was some sort of penance."

A chill seeped into his skin despite the fact that he was sweating. Stavros let Dmitri go. "What if she hasn't changed? What if she…"

"Give her a chance at least, Stavros. To prove you right or wrong."

It was Dmitri that finally left the room.

Everything Dmitri had said was stuff he had already been over a thousand times.

The moment Dmitri had called him, guilt had clung to Stavros.

All his life, he had tried to do his duty by his grandparents, by Calista, by Giannis. He hadn't let his own fears or wants matter. He had always done the right thing. He knew what he had to do now, knew Leah deserved a chance. And yet, he wavered, for the first time in his life.

Never had his mind or body been so out of sync as it was now.

Five years ago, he had let his anger detract him, and now the intensity of his want for her was a weakness he had never had to deal with before. He wiped his face and looked at himself in the mirror.

He had let nothing but his responsibilities, his sense of duty, guide him his entire life.

Nothing was going to change that, not his reckless, selfish, brazen wife of all people in the world.

CHAPTER FOUR

STANDING AT THE small balcony that offered a view of the colorful Athens evening ahead, Leah looked out.

She had been running for the past hour, the one thing that had always grounded her. Yet, all she felt like was running away, and this time, not looking back.

The panic-fueled urge was like an itch under her skin, a fire in her nerves.

It was a quarter past five and already the cafes and eateries were filling up with locals and tourists alike. Laughter and excited phrases in Greek swirled up through the air. It was a sight that had brought her a smile countless number of times after another long, lonely day. Today, it couldn't dispel her anxiety even a little bit.

Sighing, she went back inside. The pristine white walls that she had refused to adorn with even a single photo closed in on her and she started pacing.

Why hadn't she run away before now? Why hadn't she walked away from Stavros and this…pitiful thing between them that was a marriage, and not looked back?

Had she been so lonely to cling to this familiar world even knowing that she could never be close to her grandfather in the way it mattered? Had even Stavros's punishment been better than facing a life alone in the world?

She would never forgive herself for the part she had played in it, but, to this day, she had no idea that Calista had been using. Had no idea that hiding Calista's involvement in everything Stavros had abhorred about Leah would go that far.

Had no idea what it was about Stavros that made the worst parts of her manifest so well.

Impulse and fear making her movements jerky, she reached her closet and pulled out a shoulder bag that had collected dust from sitting unused for so long. Grabbed a few clothes and threw them in the bag.

For two days, she had waited calmly, taking Philip's advice to not do anything rash. Had waited for the explosion from Stavros to come. Had barely slept a wink, was driving herself crazy.

She couldn't wait to see if Stavros would take her bait. She would have to cut her ties, beginning with this flat and her job.

Just as she grabbed her phone, it pinged and the name Stavros popped up on her screen.

Leah dropped it with a gasp, her heart jamming in her throat. Perspiration condensed on her forehead as she stared down at the phone on the dull carpet.

It pinged again, jolting her out of her haze. She swiped it open to the text.

Come down to the café in ten minutes. I have an offer for you.

An offer? Could she trust him? Had she finally got through to him?

Will scream if I see your 'security guys.'

She waited, her breath hanging in her throat.

Enough drama, Leah. Come down or I come upstairs.

The thought of Stavros invading her private space, as much of a jail as it was, sent her fingers flying over the phone.

Fine, see you in a bit.

Feeling more hopeful than she'd been in months, she was about to step into the shower when it pinged again.

Leah...Dress appropriately.

Leaning against the bathroom wall, she made an utterly juvenile face at the phone. The small space thundered with the boom of her heart.

Stavros was here because he had bought her bluff. It wouldn't do to let on how petrified she was inside, to let him set the tone for this conversation.

It was like a mask she had to wear and the more she did it, the more it felt like she would become that uncaring, selfish person that he had always despised.

He had said ten minutes.

By the time he spied her crossing the street from her building to the café, it was well over half an hour. In true Leah form, she had also blatantly disregarded his last text.

The peach-colored silk blouse pressed against her body, neatly delineating the globes of her high breasts as a gust of wind blew across the street. He saw her shiver and grab the edges of the long-sleeved cardigan together.

Heat uncoiled under his own skin, a soft, sinuous gathering of something molten.

The silk blouse was paired with an even more flimsy pair of shorts that showcased her long legs. The glint of a toned thigh muscle, the way her wavy brown hair swept into a high ponytail swung with her long-limbed stride as she walked toward the café in her knee-high leather boots turned more than one male head.

She walked with the innate grace of an athlete, confident in her own skin. There was nothing of the Leah he had married and not because she had grown into her beauty. It was like a fire burned within, one that made her something to behold.

Was it truly as she had claimed and about her career? Or was it a man? Every cell in him went on high alert at the thought.

The last man Leah had been close with had been a crook of the first order—Alex Ralston, who was in jail even now for possession and distribution of drugs.

"When will you learn that defying me only wrecks your own life, Leah?" he said, dragging her down to the seat next to him.

Crossing her legs in a languorous gesture, she curved her pink-glossed mouth in a too sweet smile. "When will you learn that you cannot order me around, Stavros?"

As silky soft as her skin had been to the touch, her pulse had been pounding a thousand beats a minute. She was nervous. And yet, she was doing everything she could to not let him see it.

He waved away the waiter that arrived at their table with a beaming smile for her.

She waved him back with a friendly smile. When he glared at her, she sighed.

"*I am* hungry, Stavros. I rarely, if ever, eat out so I'm going to pretend you enjoy my company and make the most of it."

He waited in silence as the young waiter appeared again. Watched in mounting fascination as she ordered three appetizers and two entrees in fractured but perfectly accurate Greek.

"I'm not eating," he said dismissively as the waiter left.

"I know. It's Friday evening and you'll have dinner

with Helene Petrou, ex-lover and—" a curse flew from his mouth "—current *friend*."

Leaning forward in an elegant move, he pinned her gaze. "How do you know about that?"

"Philip has his resources."

"So your little lawyer asked you to casually throw that into the conversation?"

"Actually, quite the opposite. He told me not to even betray the fact that I knew anything about her," she said with that blunt and reckless honesty.

Stavros settled back slowly.

Leah had zero self-preservation. How was he supposed to believe that she could look after herself?

"Then why did you?"

"I don't want to wage a war against you, Stavros. It's… my last choice. I bring it up because I was…shocked to hear her name after so many years. That you see her apparently on a weekly basis."

"Shocked to learn that I keep in touch with a woman I admire?" he said, choosing his words carefully.

Looking anywhere but at him, she nodded. The fine sheen of color in her cheeks snagged his attention.

Brazen, reckless Leah was uncomfortable?

"I remembered that Calista…she talked so much about you guys. That you were made for each other," she said, her gaze wandering off into the distance.

The look in her eyes was a compelling blend of pain and ache that Stavros had never seen before. Did she truly mourn Calista that much? "Leah?"

She blinked and then curved her mouth. But the artifice of the action wasn't lost to him. "You would be free. To be with her."

"You want me to be with Helene?" he said, shocked.

"Yes." She took a sip of water, her gaze lingering on him. "Of course, I would prefer it if you were as miserable as you've always made me, but if your happiness is the price of my freedom…then so be it."

"That's very magnanimous of you, Leah." The whole conversation was twistedly perverse. "I'm surprised you remember her. Or anything from that time."

His dig bounced off her. "Her resume is far too impressive to forget. Businesswoman, fashion icon, former model and the best of all, the one who could stand up to Stavros Sporades's infinitely impeccable standards for a woman."

He stared at the almost cynical twist of her mouth, something in her tone grating at him. "You have quite the opinion about her."

"Of course, I do. I was obsessed with…" Coloring, she trailed her gaze away from him. "How successful she was at such a young age."

He had a curious feeling that it wasn't what she meant to say. If he compartmentalized his abhorrence for everything Leah represented and his unwise awareness of her every move, he could admit that Leah was funny and resilient as hell.

The more he pondered that, the more he realized how true it was.

Despite losing her father suddenly in a car accident and being thrust into an unfamiliar world that Giannis and he lived in, he had never seen her morose or down.

That same selfishness that he abhorred also lent her a strange strength. It was as if she stood behind a veil that separated her emotions, her very self from the people around her.

"So was all that food to please the waiter?"

"Where are your manners, Stavros?"

"All my finer qualities disappear like a mist when it comes to you, Leah."

"I was running this afternoon. So *all* that food is for me."

Stavros nodded, understanding the toned litheness of

her body. "What happened to walking out the flat and the job? To letting your little lawyer loose on me?"

He saw her still for a second before she turned toward him. "I… Philip advised me to not do anything rash."

"And you listened." Which meant she trusted him, which meant Stavros needed to know everything about him.

The waiter brought the food and she grabbed a fork. A satisfied sound erupted from her mouth, drawing the gaze and attention of more than one man sitting at the neighboring tables.

She looked up from her food suddenly and blushed. "So what is your offer?"

"I'm proposing a compromise."

"Nothing you ever suggest is a compromise. It will be your will, only couched in deceptive words. You did the same thing to…"

At the sudden glint in his gaze, Leah fiddled with the fork and looked away.

"To whom?"

Her shrimp suddenly tasted like sawdust in her mouth. Leah swallowed it down with a sip of her water. "To me and Calista, of course, countless times. Anything she proposed, you forbade it."

Like the time when she had wanted to study art in Paris one year, and when she had wanted to travel to New York with Leah. Like the time when Calista had wanted to start bartending at a nightclub where her friend had worked.

And when he refused her, one of Calista's rages would begin. Just the memory rattled Leah on a deep level. Calista had had a temper but she had hidden it so thoroughly from her brother.

"For instance?" he added softly, and Leah blinked. "You looked so pained just now, tell me what you were thinking, Leah."

The inherent command rankled Leah, and yet, beneath

it, she sensed his eagerness, his curiosity. That there could be more to Stavros than rules and duty…it threw her.

He had only been in his twenties when she had arrived in Athens, and yet, all she remembered about Stavros was his incredible sense of responsibility and duty toward all of them.

For the first time, she wondered what drove him to it.

Her curiosity tempered her response. "Why do you want to know?"

He blinked now, as if he couldn't believe that she dared question him. No, it wasn't that. Dumbfounded, she watched as he struggled to put his thoughts into words. "I… Even though I gave her everything she could ever want, I never understood—" something in her loosened as he visibly swallowed "—why Calista chose to follow your lead, how I failed to protect her."

The anguish in his gaze sent memories and impressions hurtling through Leah. Her shoulders shook. "I don't know—"

"Not that I expect you to know the answer, when you're the one who led her to drugs."

Her head jerked up.

Arrogant implacability wreathed his features. As if he had realized who he was talking to. As if there could be nothing but contempt between them.

"No, of course not," she whispered, buffeting herself against the immense hurt his words caused. Leah put her fork down.

Despite all her grand plans and ideas for adventures, Calista had never even lifted a finger in the house. Whereas Leah, whose mother had died giving birth to her, had always done more than her share to help out her dad even from a young age.

My saintly brother has servants for that… It had been her favorite thing to say when Leah would suggest cleaning up or cooking sometimes.

She had been sixteen and afraid and grieving in her own way. How much of her understanding of Calista would hold up today? For a minute, it seemed she and Stavros had found something common in their grief over Calista.

But no, the past was done. She had to look forward to the future.

Collecting herself, Leah looked up at him. "Tell me what I have to do."

He studied her for the longest time. Each falling second twisted her gut. "Live with me for three months and prove that I can trust you."

"No." The table rattled with the force of her movement.

"This is the only way I will even consider it."

"What do you expect me to do these three months?"

"Convince me that you're serious about this fashion design career, that you won't drain your inheritance on some trumped-up business."

"The vote of confidence in your tone is really inspiring."

That hardness in his eyes didn't budge. "I'm giving you a real choice. If you fail, our marriage stands. You'll be my wife in every sense for as long as one of us is alive."

A violent tremble started at the base of her spine and spread upward and outward. The happy voices around her buzzed as if they were noise feedback. And in that space between them, a charge built up winding and changing with every breath they took.

Leah struggled against it, rationalized against it. He met his lover every week. He could not be attracted to her. Nor she to him.

This charge was antagonism that had gone unaddressed for so many years, hatred and resentment and their struggle against this very fate that was spilling over into something else. Maybe it would be true if she believed it enough, she thought desperately.

Because thinking of Stavros in this way—when even

her juvenile crush on him had always left her feeling inadequate, was the last thing she needed in life.

Through sheer will, she forced herself to break his gaze, to focus on the fact that he was giving her a real chance. That Giannis would be far removed from their deal was positive.

"If I do prove that I'm everything that is virtuous and sweet and biddable and completely without personality?" His scowl deepened and since needling Stavros was the only thing she had control over in the sinking confusion of her world, she continued, "I'm just a little bit worried that you might not want to give me up then."

His laughter clanged in the open café. It was a sound Leah had so rarely heard that she stared at him, her breath caught somewhere in her throat.

That lean chest rumbled as if he couldn't contain it. From the long column of his throat to the sharp grooves in his sliced cheeks...he was gorgeous to behold.

It seemed the café froze around them to take in the sight.

A woman at the next table stilled with her coffee cup halfway to her mouth, her gaze eating him up. Still laughing, he pushed back the thick lock of jet-black hair that fell onto his forehead.

And the solid gold band on his finger glinted in the streetlight.

The twinkle of the metal struck Leah in the chest as if it were an arrow.

The wedding band... He was wearing his wedding band?

The ring she had slipped onto his finger while tears had pooled in her eyes. The ring that had bound her to him in the holiest of bonds and yet was nothing but a shackle...

Why did he wear the damned ring? Had he worn it that day aboard Dmitri's yacht?

Had he worn it over the past five years?

Anxiety rippled over her, like a flurry of ants had skittered over her skin.

Just like her, the woman's gaze also fell on the ring and then shifted to encompass the both of them. Leah felt her curiosity like a prickle, could see her trying to calculate where Leah fit into Stavros's life.

Nowhere, Leah reminded herself. That he wore that ring was probably nothing but a reminder of his duty to Giannis.

Did he keep it on when he made love to the regal Helene? What would it be like to be the woman he respected, he adored, the woman he promised his utter devotion to? Would his passion run just as deep as his sense of duty?

"Even in the most unlikely chance that I find you that irresistible…" Utter mockery resonated in every word, crashing her down. "I will sign the divorce papers, release your inheritance. You'll be free."

Three months with Stavros…

"The freedom to live my life as I want is my basic right. I shouldn't have to prove anything for it nor should I have to threaten…nor do I have to do despicable things."

"So you're not completely without conscience?"

She refused to answer that when he was the one who had pushed her to it. "You're not the lord of my life."

"Apparently, I am. And you lost all rights to your own life when you threatened it by living so recklessly." His very stillness as his gaze burned with frustration was disconcerting. "*Theos*, Leah…Calista died and Giannis almost did because of the heart attack you gave him. How can you sit there and defend yourself?"

"I can defend myself because…" Clutching the metal edge of the table, Leah breathed deeply. His accusation was unfair, so wrong, and yet, the guilt it brought was no less suffocating.

And to dig into the past, to tell him the truth would mean exposing herself to a man who tolerated no weakness, knew no fears.

Would he laugh at her as he had done just now or pity her?

So she gave in. "Fine. I'll do as you demand and earn that right back."

Silence met her acceptance.

He hadn't expected her to give in so quickly. Did he think it was an admission of guilt?

His arrogance that he knew everyone and the best for everyone had riled her from day one. Not once had he tried to figure out what or how she had felt. He'd only made assumptions, and then ordered her around.

He dropped some bills on the table, and extended his hand for her. "Let's pick up what you need for a few days. The movers will bring the rest of your belongings later."

Panic ran free in her gut as Leah shook her head. "No. I...I can't just pack up everything I need in ten minutes. I need a few days."

She couldn't just move in with him in a matter of hours. She needed to get used to the idea first. Needed to get her head screwed on right.

He checked the glinting Rolex on his wrist and then looked back at her. "I'll have someone come by to give us a hand. In the meantime, we can get started."

"You're actually, physically going to help me pack?"

"Is that a problem?"

"Yes, of course it is," she sputtered, refusing his outstretched hand. "I don't want you in my...I just... The flat is a mess, and you'll instantly judge me and tell me I shouldn't be allowed to live by myself or some such nonsense."

The hateful man had the gall to smile at her. To actually smile, showing his perfectly even teeth and the dimple in one cheek that should have made him look effeminate yet only added to that austere masculinity.

"What if I tell you that housekeeping is not a criterion I'll count?"

Desperation coated her throat. "I...I'm not comfortable with others touching my personal stuff."

"Neither am I about welcoming you to my estate..."

With his hand at her elbow, he made it imperative for her to stand up. "I won't touch anything. You can pack and I'll supervise."

"You'll lord it over me, you mean?" she said, using sarcasm to hide the trembling beneath.

In all the years she had known him, he had, in turns, aggravated her, captivated her and in the end, had ended up ruling over her life. And that was when there was no direct relationship between them.

How was she supposed to survive through three months of living with him?

CHAPTER FIVE

SHE HAD BEEN lying blatantly, *of course*.

Stavros didn't know what shocked him more. The fact that she would tell such a white lie about something so trivial or the reality of her lifeless, joyless flat.

It was as if she had intentionally designed herself a sterile prison cell, had punished herself.

Everything inside him recoiled that she had lived like this for five years. Why? Why live as though she was punishing herself when she had argued with him so furiously that she wanted it to end?

Had Calista's death scared her so much? Had it really changed her?

There was not a single thing out of place in the living room, or the small kitchen, or in the glimpse he had caught of her bedroom. She had everything she required.

The cupboards were full of silverware; a plasma television adorned the wall in the living room, yet was coated with five layers of dust.

There were no decorative items, no knickknacks. Just the bare essentials wherever he looked. The walls were a pristine white exactly as he had remembered from five years ago, when he had inspected the building and the flat, a week after they had married.

It screamed of loneliness, detachment.

Leah was a firestorm and it seemed only a ghost of that girl lived here.

The first year and a few months into the second after she had come to live here, he had had things delivered to her. Boxes of clothes and shoes, handbags and other accessories Helene had told him a young woman would require. He had even sent her things that had once belonged to her mother, found when he and Dmitri had gone through Giannis's old estate after his heart attack...

But she had sent every box back, stubbornly refusing to accept any of it, and so he had stopped trying. Even the box with her mother's things.

He had, conveniently, shrugged off his duty toward her. To the point of ignoring her very existence.

His gut twisting into a tight, unforgiving knot, he followed her into her bedroom. There was a nightstand next to the bed. A tissue box, some pencils and loose paper, and a tiny photograph of her father, he assumed from the same brown eyes, were on it.

Stretching on her toes, she pulled a bag out of her closet that was already half full. Turned around and stilled as he stayed at the entrance.

"I have someone bringing up boxes. Not that it seems you need any."

"The work room has lots of stuff I need."

He nodded and waited, his thoughts in an unprecedented jumble.

"I don't have to stay in your house for this...this test of yours, Stavros. I could just continue here."

He prowled into the small room, feeling on edge. He was angry at himself, he realized slowly. And he was angry at her. It was irrational, and yet he couldn't loosen its grip over him.

"Why not?" The taunt in his words shamed him.

The brown of her eyes transforming into a dazzling color, she glared at him. Her pulse at the neck fluttered belying the anger in her eyes. "Because I don't think it's a good idea.

CHAPTER FIVE

SHE HAD BEEN lying blatantly, *of course*.

Stavros didn't know what shocked him more. The fact that she would tell such a white lie about something so trivial or the reality of her lifeless, joyless flat.

It was as if she had intentionally designed herself a sterile prison cell, had punished herself.

Everything inside him recoiled that she had lived like this for five years. Why? Why live as though she was punishing herself when she had argued with him so furiously that she wanted it to end?

Had Calista's death scared her so much? Had it really changed her?

There was not a single thing out of place in the living room, or the small kitchen, or in the glimpse he had caught of her bedroom. She had everything she required.

The cupboards were full of silverware; a plasma television adorned the wall in the living room, yet was coated with five layers of dust.

There were no decorative items, no knickknacks. Just the bare essentials wherever he looked. The walls were a pristine white exactly as he had remembered from five years ago, when he had inspected the building and the flat, a week after they had married.

It screamed of loneliness, detachment.

Leah was a firestorm and it seemed only a ghost of that girl lived here.

"You can't stand me, for sins I know and some I don't. And I...you're arrogant, you're a hypocrite and I..." she said with that standard animosity she seemed to reserve especially for him. Yet he heard the quiver beneath those words.

She was trying so hard to hide her awareness of him. So hard to fight it.

The Leah that he knew, *that he thought he had known*, had never fought anything she felt. Gave in to every juvenile urge, every self-serving impulse until she crashed and burned.

And had dragged Calista down with her.

This effort now...it sparked a curious fire in him just as much as the fluttering pulse at her neck did.

He came to her bed and leaned against it, blocking her. "So that you could continue to live in this hole like some damned martyr?"

A silk skirt in hand, she turned that gaze to him again. "It is what you chose for me."

"I never meant for you to live like a prisoner. I sent you everything you needed."

"To do what with?" Throwing the skirt and a couple more things into the bag, she zipped it up vehemently. "I have no friends, Stavros. No family..."

"You rejected the one you have for years. You still do," he couldn't help but point out, a gnawing frustration in his gut.

She didn't even flinch as she continued. "Even the staff at the fashion house, people I have been working with for five years, they treat me with this—" he saw her swallow and a wave of tenderness, shocking and acute, rose inside him "—nauseating combination of dislike and affected regard.

"I don't know if they think my designs are really good or if they are just saying that because I'm Leah Sporades, the wife of the textile magnate of Greece, a shame he hides from the world.

"You married me even though you despised the sight of me. You...you kissed me in front of the media that day for the express purpose of warning away my friends, the entire world. You might as well have branded me like they do livestock."

"Leah—"

"No, Stavros...I was nineteen. I lost the one friend I had, Giannis had just had a heart attack..."

"Whom you still refuse to see," he cut in.

Do not give up on my Leah, Stavros. Please...she is very fragile...

Fragile was the last thing he had ever thought of Leah... She had barely ever sat down for five minutes with him, yet even surrounded by tubes and equipment, she'd been all Giannis could think about.

Every inch of her slender frame vibrating with anger and pain, she clutched the lapels of his shirt. "...and in the next two days, you took my entire world away from me. You locked me up here and promptly forgot about me.

"Did you ever feel even an ounce of shame that you co-erced a nineteen-year-old into marriage?"

Stavros felt her words dig into him like the serrated edge of a blade, drawing blood.

For five years, he had ignored her very existence, had let her live like this, had informed Giannis again and again that Leah was well...

How had he committed such an unforgivable mistake?

"Answer me."

"No, I don't regret it. I would have done anything to save you from that drug-induced-drink-all-night-reckless-party life."

No denial rushed out of her this time. Instead, she closed her eyes and bent her head to his chest. The raw intimacy of the gesture flayed him, reaching a part he didn't know he possessed.

Her shoulders pushing at his chest, the scent of her coating the air he breathed, her lithe form was so tempting. He wanted to wrap his arms around her, he wanted to bury his mouth in… Feeling like an iron anvil was sitting on his chest, he clasped her wrists to push her away.

Instead, the pad of his thumb moved over the plump vein of its own will.

Her breaths came in a slow rasp until, suddenly, she looked up. His lungs burned for air as her fingers laced around his, as a blunt nail raked the center of his palm, her molten brown gaze clung to his lips.

Something so desperate and wanting flashed in her gaze that Stavros dropped her hand.

It was so unlike Leah that a shiver raked down his spine.

Jerking away from him, she drew a deep breath. "Deal with the consequences of what you did then," she said, moving her hand over the room. "Alleviating your guilt about this…it's not my responsibility."

It was the most adult thing she had ever said to him. And just like that, his world tilted an infinitesimal inch.

A world in which Leah was right and he was wrong. A world in which he had let himself be led by pain and resentment until he had neglected his duty…neglected the vow he had made to Giannis.

"You're right. It's not."

"What?"

"I said you're right," he said willingly, the bright wonder on her face drawing it out of him. "What I did that day had consequences that I didn't own completely."

"Am I actually hearing this?" Her brows rose into her hair, her mouth opened in a long O. Mirth overflowed in those eyes, making her look absolutely stunning. *"Boom!"* The scent of her skin swirled around him, drugging him so insidiously that his blood became sluggish. "Did you hear that, Stavros? I think the sky just exploded…"

He stole another greedy look at her. And like a snake

waiting to strike, the most incredible urge to press his thumb against the lushness of her lower lip, struck him.

He collected himself slowly and stepped out, wondering if this sinuous desire for her was his true penance.

"Show me your workroom," he said, over his shoulder.

Her workroom knocked the breath out of Stavros.

It was as though a veil, the veil that separated Leah from the rest of them, had been lifted. A tentative smile on her face, she walked around touching things here and there in the chaotic room, eons different from the Leah who usually glared at him with such hatred.

Sunlight poured in streams into the high-ceilinged room, exposing the beams. Everywhere he looked, there was color, such a vivid contrast to the rest of the apartment that it took him a few moments to actually see it.

Two racks hung around the back, with evening gowns in different degrees of completion. An old sewing machine lay on a table in the other corner. One whole wall was covered with sketches made in pencil, illustrations, even cut-outs from fashion magazines.

Swatches of fabric were pasted on another wall. Reams of it spilled over from a rickety shelf in the corner—satin and silk and cotton, pretty much every fabric he knew of in his ten years in the textile industry.

Something tightened in his chest.

"The retail buyer that you were talking about, what is she interested in?"

"I'm putting together a collection of evening wear for her—cocktail dresses, formal gowns, and the prize of the collection will be one bridal dress."

"That's quite a workload for one designer…"

"Slash seamstress," she finished, fingering the sheer fabric of one unfinished dress.

"You're going to…"

An utterly confident smile dawned on her face. "Actually cut and sew the dresses, yes. I custom-design and sew every dress myself and that's what I would like my brand to be. When the buyer was talking about what she would like, what she liked about my previous designs...I could see the concept from start to finish."

Color flushed her skin.

He walked around and touched the cut bodice in ivory silk. "Has she seen the flat sketches?"

She shook her head. And he saw the surprise in her eyes that he knew the term. "We have had two discussions around it."

"Leah, it's a huge risk to create an entire collection for one woman's tastes at this stage."

She tilted her jaw aggressively. "You gave me your word not ten minutes ago." Her lithe frame vibrated with her growing panic.

"And I will stand by it. But I'm also a businessman and in case, you have forgotten, I run a group of textile factories that export all over the world. All I'm doing is pointing out the pitfalls, as I would do with any business I want to invest in. Creatives have a tendency to run the business into the ground with their half-realized dreams."

"But I'm not creating exactly what she wants. More like my vision of what she has in mind." She turned to him, a frown on her face. "Anything I tried to design with some freedom at the fashion house ends up changed for the brand of the house. I want this collection to be mine. And I need cash upfront for all the raw materials."

He nodded. "I want an expense report including quotes from all the vendors you'll be sourcing the raw material from. I want every penny accounted for."

"I will send you my spreadsheet."

"You have one already?"

"Surprised, aren't you? I've been having problems with one vendor based in Brazil though. He keeps upping the price of the cotton I need from him."

"I can help with that," he said, the fire in her eyes stunning him. "Do you plan to hire another seamstress?"

"Not at this point."

"But it's too much work for just one person."

"I don't want anyone else involved in this...in my first collection."

"Fine," he said, noting that the stubborn streak of independence was still there. Also that whatever advice he gave now, she wouldn't heed it. "You'll have the money within the hour. I will be gone next week, and during that time—"

Walking back into the kitchen, she pulled a bottle of water from the fridge. "I'll be watched by your housekeeper and your new security head. Poor Dmitri, along with his arm candies, will be reduced to babysitting duties. Although, I don't mind him."

"No?" The question left his mouth before he knew he had thought it.

"Dmitri?" An almost dazed kind of smile glimmered in her expression. And he cut the irrationally possessive thought her expression evoked before it could form fully. "Of course not. He was always kind, even when Calista..." Sudden tension dawned in her gaze and she looked away from him.

"When Calista what, Leah?"

She cleared her throat and started again but resolutely kept her gaze away from him. "This one time, we snuck into his room and stole a bottle of whiskey. Only he caught us..."

"Whiskey, Leah?"

"We were just goofing around, Stavros. We were seventeen."

"My father was an alcoholic who stole from his own parents, sold our house just so that he could drink, and drove my mother away. Calista wasn't supposed to even touch that stuff."

Shock flared in her gaze, widening those beautiful eyes.

Only then did he realize how much he had betrayed. "I had no idea, Stavros."

"What did he do, Leah?"

"Oh, he told us we could drink the whiskey—" color stole into her cheeks and she wouldn't meet his eyes "—as long as we were also going to join him for a threesome after."

"*Cristo!* Of all the things to say to—"

As if expecting his reaction, Leah sighed. "We dropped the bottle where we stood and we ran, Stavros. Dmitri was used to…he knew how to deal with us."

Unlike you, her unsaid accusation screamed.

He had a feeling Dmitri definitely understood Leah far better than he did. A mistake he had to rectify…

If Giannis had asked me… He pushed away the scenario provoked by Dmitri's taunting remark from his head and focused his mind on practicalities.

"Leah…fashion design is extremely hard to break into. On a given day, there are tens, if not hundreds, of designers launching new labels. And I don't know whether you actually have any talent for this."

"I know that. All I'm asking is a chance to do it, to access the resources that I do have."

"And when—" he checked himself as she threw that trademark glare at him "—*if* you fail in this venture?"

"Then it will be my failure. All mine. Just as the success would be. It will be something I have put my heart and joy into, something that doesn't scare me."

"I thought nothing scared you, Leah."

She offered him a perfunctory smile, and Stavros realized how much he didn't know about the girl he had thought his bitterest penance.

CHAPTER SIX

A WEEK LATER, Leah walked over the white sandy beach on Stavros's estate on one of the tiny islands along the Aegean coast. Stavros's "house" turned out to be a hundred-acre estate close to the sea, a ten-minute helicopter ride from Athens that had thrilled her quite a bit.

Even with Stavros studying her curiously the whole time.

She had lived in Athens for so many years and yet she had known nothing about the little slice of heaven that was the island he called home.

Nestled amidst two tiny hills, the mansion was stunning in its simplicity. No glittering glass bars like Dmitri's yacht, or a lifeless steel-and-chrome affair, which was lately the trend with billionaire homes.

The manor was made entirely of stone, with cathedral ceilings framed by exposed beams, whitewashed walls, a pool and a wine cellar. It was full of soaring spaces and light, stunning in its simple lines.

Austere, private and yet so breathtaking, the exact reflection of the man who owned it, it was an authentic slice of rural Greece. But even when it was only the wind chimes that punctured the silence, even when it was just the staff keeping her company as it had been at the apartment, Leah felt anything but lonely.

There was something very peaceful about the estate and the people surrounding it.

She smiled now about how worried she had been about

being confined in a house with him. About seeing Stavros wherever she turned. Not only did the house boast seven bedrooms and attached baths, but Stavros, when he returned from Katrakis Textiles, she realized, worked in the estate.

Although if he had looked smolderingly arrogant in his suit, he looked painfully handsome in light blue jeans and a white polo shirt.

The sounds of the helicopter blades had jolted her from her bed the first morning. Still in her cotton shorts and sleeveless T-shirt, she had run to the attached balcony, spurred on by what, she still didn't know.

Dressed in a white dress shirt that draped lovingly over his broad frame and plain khaki trousers that looked way too sexy, he had been about to step in.

Except he had turned and looked at her, the breeze ruffling his hair.

Her heart thudding, her mouth dry, Leah had broken his gaze and gone back in.

Now returning from the beach, she waved at workers heading home to the small village from the vineyard, which she had been surprised to learn was operational. Several guesthouses were dotted across the grounds in addition to a horse farm.

When she had laughingly asked Stavros which one Dmitiri preferred when he visited, she had gotten a black look in response.

It was as she passed a couple, probably in their fifties, that she remembered another little tidbit. Stavros and Calista had been from a little village that surrounded Stavros's estate. His grandparents, she knew, still lived there. Even though their grandson was a household name in all of Greece.

Feeling nauseous at the thought of how brazenly she had threatened to go to the media and how his face had blazed in contempt, she pulled in a long breath and broke into a run.

From the moment he had showed her around the estate, she had loved running through the trails cleared through lush acreage. In just the past week, she had found a trail that touched the horse farm and rounded through the orchard.

She turned the winding bend around it and came to a skidding halt near the glittering pool that was by the house.

The evening sun kissing the bridge of his nose and his cheekbones, Stavros was sitting at the poolside table.

A tall jug of the customary lemonade that she requested every day and a selection of fruits and assorted cheeses were on the glass-topped table between the two loungers.

His head was thrown back against it, and his eyes were closed. Her breathing still raspy, Leah stilled. Her gaze lingering on the corded column of his throat, the planes of his sculpted face, at the way his long lashes almost kissed those sharp cheekbones…

It was something to see the man in repose like that, to study him without his contemptuous gaze peeling layers off her. And the way her breath hitched and her gut folded, the frenzied clamoring of her heartbeat to the very sight of him, it was telling.

For the past week, she had seen the stamp of the man in the thriving estate.

In the tired but happy workers on the vineyard, in the affluent praise the villagers bestowed on him, in the way some of the women's eyes had widened when they had realized who she was, the reverence in their tone when they addressed her as Thespinis Sporades…

The responsibility of bearing that name, the reality of being the woman Stavros would respect and know *and want*…it sent shivers down her spine.

The usual white dress shirt he wore was unbuttoned, showing dark olive skin. His cuffs, folded back, displayed his muscled forearms, to the veins extending from his wrist and down… The sight of those powerful thighs, encased in tight blue jeans, made her remember how hard and corded they had been against her own…made her wonder how they would cradle her if she…

Heat, that had nothing to do with her running, pooled under her skin. The stretchy fabric of her Lycra top rasped against her nipples, the soft hem of her shorts rubbing against her inner thighs…

She was breathing like she had run another few laps, her skin so overheated that dunking into the pool was so inviting. Just as she found her willpower and took a step, she heard her name.

Turning slowly, she saw his fingers laced against his chest, faint color bleeding into those cheekbones.

His eyes were still closed when he said, "Did you have a good week, Leah?"

He sounded hoarse, uneven. Very unlike him. *Had he felt the way her gaze devoured him in that motionless state?*

How could just looking at him fill her blood with this molten wanting?

"Come, sit here and tell me how it was," he said softly.

While she still stood there stupidly, hovering between drugged inertia and fluttering panic, his gaze opened slowly. Traveled over her with such a thorough intensity that she could almost believe he had been dying to look at her.

In the seconds-long perusal, Leah knew he had noted everything about her, including her heightened color. Hoped he would put it down to the fact that she had been running.

She ran her palm over her forehead, wondering if she was feverish. Because that's how she felt. Could a harmless, adolescent crush turn into a full-fledged obsession, she thought sarcastically. "I'm sweaty. I need a shower," she finally responded, and began to walk away.

"Rosa told me you like to swim after your run. Don't change your routine on my account. Or am I one of those incredible things that scare you, Leah?"

It was so on target that her denial shot out of her mouth like a missile in a defensive tone. "I'm not afraid of you."

His brows rose questioningly. Then he smiled, a real flicker of warmth lighting up those tawny irises.

She could deal with Stavros hating her, questioning her worth, and thinking the absolute worst of her. This... strangely speculative mood he seemed to be in, she couldn't.

No way was she going to put on her bikini and parade in front of him. She would probably self-combust if he so much as looked at her, even innocently. "I ran far more than I intended today. I'll skip the swim," she said, turning around.

"How do you like the estate?"

She was so wired up into his every breath, every nuance that her foot slipped on a wet patch.

He was out of the chair and by her side in a flash, his hand around her waist. The side of her breasts squished against him, her midriff knocked hard against his. All of her breath jarred into her throat, her muscles groaning at the impact. He was so hard and hot...

"You are unhurt?"

"I'm fine." She pushed the words out, feeling so out of control that tears prickled behind her eyes.

What was the matter with her? Where was this desperate awareness stemming from?

He was silent next to her, his large hands still resting on her hips. She didn't have the guts to turn and meet his gaze.

The idea of seeing the same awareness in his drove her out of her skin. The idea of seeing nothing but a patient indifference made her skin crawl.

With the guise of reaching for the lemonade, she withdrew from his touch. "It's remote and a little out of sync with the twenty-first century, don't you think?"

For the first time in years, she had felt completely at home, had forgotten the pain of the past and the endless, lonely future stretching ahead of her. But she had nothing to fight her reaction with, if not with her lies. Nothing except to continue the animosity between them that she didn't even know the origins of anymore.

"Remote, yes. Out of sync with the rest of the world, no."

She looked at him over the rim of her glass. "Perfect for you though—stark, severe and forbidding."

"That's exactly what Dmitri says when he visits. Says he can't stand the relentless silence." He smiled. "So you do not like it then?"

She frowned, wondering why he was asking. "I just... I prefer something a little flashier and more hip, like Dmitri's yacht. Or that infamous bachelor pad of his in the business district of Athens." When had lying become this easy? She had been to Dmitri's flat once and it had been a soulless, colorless monstrosity of steel and chrome. "This is a bit too isolated for my taste."

"Is it?"

She swallowed the lump in her throat at the thought of leaving here. But if this was how she was going to react to seeing him after a week, she couldn't imagine what she would do if she saw him daily. "Hmmm."

A little knot tied his brows and cleared again. Something she had never seen danced in the depths of his gaze.

He was going to relent. He was going to send her back to that dinky flat, back to the dragon, Mrs. Kovlakis. A breeze could have knocked her down at how desperately sad the thought made her.

Dark gaze unmoving from her, he finished her drink. She looked down, rattled by the intimacy of the gesture. He put the glass down slowly and wiped his mouth while she waited on edge. "I think I will choose not to believe you, *agape mou*."

The endearment ripped through her. It meant nothing to him but weaved an intimacy that she didn't know how to counter. "What...what do you mean?"

"You are lying." The announcement reverberated around them in the vast space. He didn't sound angry though. "I probably have been arrogant enough in the past to take everything you said on face value. Even made it easy for you to manipulate me, *ne*? The why of it, I have not learned it *yet*." A promise, that he would find out sooner or later, resonated in his tone.

"I think you love the estate. I barely took my jeep out when I got stopped so many times today. Everyone already knew your name, everyone had tales to tell about you. Rosa," he said, coming closer, "even said she had never met such a hardworking and lovely young woman."

Leah frowned, as if trying to keep her shock out of her face. "Of course, I was forced to be nice to her. Your housekeeper is an evil genius that bewitched me with that decadent dark coffee and servings of baklava."

"The important question is how many things have you lied about?" he continued, as if uninterrupted.

Her skin paled, leaving such a frightened look in her eyes that Stavros jerked her around to him.

Was that unwise desire that widened those beautiful eyes real?

Was the pain in her eyes when she spoke of Calista real?

The whole week that he had been gone, he had found himself running through every encounter he had ever had with Leah.

Wondered why she had done so many things he had forbidden her to do, wondered how someone who could be so rejecting and disrespectful of Giannis again and again could also turn around and mourn for his sister, Calista, for so many years.

She had lied about the apartment. She had lied today about liking the estate, a seemingly inconsequential thing that threatened nothing that she held dear.

A keening frustration spread through his veins. Like there was a pit full of dangerous truths that he had never faced and Leah held the key to it all. He forced a smile to his mouth and pressed his hand to her back.

She instantly stiffened and he gritted his jaw, fighting the shockingly strong urge to assert his right like an uncivilized thug.

Right then, it seemed he cared very little about duty, or what was right. All he wanted to do was touch her, to feel like this stranger who told him nothing but lies, that selfish, reckless girl he had married, was really present.

Right then, he wanted to claim something, a part of her, even an emotion, an expression, that no one else knew but him.

Right then, he wanted to be a self-serving bastard like Dmitri and assure himself that she would respond, even against her own surprisingly strong will, when he touched her. That she couldn't pretend, fake, or lie to him in that.

It was as if suddenly there was a beast inside him that wanted to do as it pleased, that was railing against the cage after a lifetime of doing what was right.

And it was Leah that did these things to him.

"So your lawyer friend visited you on Wednesday."

Resignation flattened the curve of her mouth. "His name is Philip." He was only a few inches taller than her, and standing a step below her, his eyes were level with her mouth.

What would she do if he touched those lush lips with his?

Would she fight him and scratch him like the alley cat she had always pretended to be? Or would she sink into his kiss as that desperate desire in her eyes suggested?

Which was the real Leah?

"He was in a foul temper because I came away with you without taking his advice. Not knowing how autocratic you can be, he thinks I gave in too easily."

Stavros wanted to figure her out, put her in a category and move on with life. He didn't want this curiosity, didn't know how to arrest this indulgent self-awareness that she incited in him.

"I think he sees his piece of pie from your fortune dwindling away."

She walked around the table like a cornered prey. "Because he befriended me with nothing but an eye toward what I'm worth?"

"Yes. Your fortune always attracts those kinds of men."

A sigh escaped her, but she wasn't spitting in fury as he had imagined. As if he were the despot she could hate again. "And of course, you know everyone and their intentions best."

"No, I know Philip Cosgrove better than you do. He has had two broken engagements—one with an American candy heiress and the other with a princess from a minor South American nation. He has also been having an affair with a client."

Hands on hips, she looked like a wildcat. "You had him investigated?"

"You should know the truth about him."

"Truth about his personal life? He's a friend and my lawyer, Stavros. Not my lover. If he was going to be one, I'm sure he would have volunteered that information. And even if he didn't, it's my decision to make."

The thought of Leah with any man...he wasn't prepared to ponder his reaction to that. "Now you know what decision to make."

"About whether I want to screw him or not?" she said crudely, even as color darkened her cheeks. "You don't have the right to police me on who I sleep with."

"Discussing my rights and privileges when it comes to you is not a conversation you will like, *agape mou*."

"No, I won't. Because you're a hypocrite. Do you tell your lovers that you have a wife you hide as if she were a stain on the very fabric of your life, Stavros?" Her fingers clutched his hand and pulled it up, a startling tremble in it.

The contact jolted through him. "Do you take it off when you undress your lover? Do you—"

"I don't have to tell them anything," he whispered, dragging her against him. She was stiff against him, yet just the drag of her body set his muscles curling with need.

Ever since she had entered his life, there had been no escape from the shackles his own sense of honor bound him with.

Strange then that he had resented it and fought it for so long.

Was it because, as he had always known, Leah would never be the kind of wife he had imagined for himself—someone calm and dependable like Helene? Even then, had he known that she would incite him to this kind of reckless, unwise need?

"Anyone who's someone knows I have a wife. Which also means I don't have to fend off women with marriage on their mind…"

She stared, unblinking. Her nostrils flared. "You're… disgusting."

It was addictive to play her own game with her, so compelling to watch the different expressions pass through her eyes. In that moment, there were no lies she could tell him. In that moment, the connection between them was as explosive and destructive as the wildfire that had wrecked through the surrounding acreage a few years ago.

A fire that was going to need feeding soon if he didn't it to want it to consume him, as it had already begun to… if he didn't want to lose all sense of right and wrong.

And what was wrong with wanting his own wife in his bed? Maybe if he gave in to the fire, he could function normally again.

"You wanted to know," he goaded her.

"No, I didn't. I was just trying to make a point."

"You sounded like a nagging, jealous wife. Just what I wanted my marriage to be."

All color fled from her face, leaving her gaze stricken. Tears pooled in her eyes. And the sight of those big brown eyes brimming with moisture punched him in the gut.

"*Theos*, Leah—"

"I hate you. I hate that you're keeping me here. I hate that you have so much power over my life and that you use it at every turn to put me in the wrong. And I'm such a pathetic coward that I still stand here, day after day, hoping that you will change your mind. I forget that all you want is to punish me, and yourself, for what happened to Calista.

"That's all this is, isn't it? Duty, righting a wrong... nothing touches you beyond that."

She cast another desperate glance at him, swiped her hands roughly over her eyes and walked away.

Her words sliced at Stavros rendering everything she said about him a lie.

It did hurt, he realized with a strange new awareness. What she said about him mattered because he hadn't meant to hurt her today. *Christos*, he had never meant to hurt Leah.

He had been powerless about her influence on Calista, he had despised her willful rejection of Giannis's love, he had resented that she had sealed his fate the moment she had walked into his life but he had never meant to hurt her.

Not even the day when he had spoken his vows to her utterly petrified form.

Yet, it seemed it was all he had ever done.

That Leah could be vulnerable when it came to him, instead of making him powerful, felt like a curse.

Giannis had saved him from a life of misery and poverty and yawning emptiness and all he had done in return was make his granddaughter's life miserable.

He wouldn't forsake his duty, but neither did he want to hurt Leah anymore.

Leah leaned against the wall in her workroom, shame ringing in her ears. She couldn't believe she had betrayed herself like that. She didn't even care that he had investigated Philip or about what he had found.

But when he had called her a *nagging, jealous* wife, it was as if she could see their future like that…as if he would never see her true self. As if he would never know the real her.

Standing up, she reached for a jug of water. Poured herself a tall drink and guzzled it down.

It couldn't matter this much, not when she would be gone soon.

She couldn't be so vulnerable to him, couldn't get so emotional. The only way to accomplish that was to accept him this way. He would watch her, hover over her, dictate her life *forever*, if she wasn't careful now.

She would give up a little now for the long run.

It wasn't as if the news of Philip's past engagements affected her.

For as long as she had understood herself, only one man had always stubbornly occupied the space in her head. And still, only one man could set her heart racing, only one man could make her hate herself that she wasn't smarter or calmer or even stronger, that she wasn't a match for him in any way.

For the next week, Leah barely slept. The retail buyer, Mrs. DuPont, set up an appointment to see what Leah had for her so far. The conversation that followed, where Leah explained to her that she was now living at Stavros's estate and her reaction to the fact that she was *that Textile Magnate's wife*, had been extremely awkward. As if suddenly Leah's worth as a designer had changed. Whether for good or bad, Leah had no idea.

Once she had heard from her, Leah had finished the sewing on the first three dresses.

Unaccountably nervous, she had snarled at Stavros yesterday for making it all so complicated.

The evening after Mrs. Dupont had called, a seamstress had arrived at her workroom. Her mouth falling open in awe, she fingered the turquoise sheer silk of the cocktail dress, had said in broken English that she loved sewing, and would Mrs. Sporades please give her work.

Having neatly been maneuvered into it, Leah had nodded. Now, she was glad she had given in to Stavros's tactics. Anna was not only talented but also enthusiastic. Having arranged the three dresses on a rack, Leah endlessly tidied the workroom, her stomach a tangle of nerves.

She had risked a lot to be able to make this ready for Mrs. DuPont, to arrive at this stage of making her dream come true.

And yet, it was Stavros's challenging gaze that stayed at the forefront of her mind. The strength of her desire to show him that she was talented, hardworking, that she had what it took to succeed, only grew.

She was determined to make him see her as his equal, in this at least.

Leah would have had her meeting with the retail buyer this afternoon.

The small nugget jolted through Stavros's subconscious like he had set up a reminder chip in his brain to go off every hour. All through his day, through numerous meetings, he found himself thinking of her, of how nervous she had been last night, of how he had seen her work long hours, only remembering to eat because Rosa threatened her.

In the last two weeks, he had found that he couldn't fault her dedication or hard work. And the night before last, learning that she had once again skipped her dinner, he had gone into her workroom.

He had found himself on her doorstep, stunned into silence as Leah commanded Anna to turn around slowly.

Being almost as tall as him, Anna was the perfect model to showcase a knee-length sheath dress in red silk.

Simple yet chic, it touched Anna with sophistication she hadn't possessed before.

Suddenly, he was extremely glad that Giannis had pushed him and Dmitri to start their work at his textile factories on the sewing floor.

In two weeks, he had learned how dedicated and hard-working she was, and in that moment, Stavros had no doubt of her talent.

It was after six by the time the helicopter touched down at his estate. A curious eagerness buffeted him like the wind from the rotor blades.

He headed directly for her workroom, seeing the light on as he approached the house.

He found her at her drawing table, one hand around her nape, turning her head this way and then other. And then her face flopped down onto her table, her shoulders trembled, and a loud, rattling sigh escaped her.

The depth of frustration in that sound startled him.

She straightened up again, tore off sheets from her sketchpad, crumpled them and tossed them.

He must have made a sound, because she suddenly turned then. "I'm so sorry, Anna, but I won't have any work for you in the near—"

In the few seconds before she realized that it was him, Stavros saw it. Distress and disappointment, which slowly cycled to wariness for him.

She slid off the high stool, holding herself stiff. "I thought it was Anna."

"How did it go?" he said, his eagerness to know unprecedented.

Folding her arms defensively, she shrugged. He saw her swallow, look away, and turn toward him again.

When she met his gaze again, she looked ready to battle him. "You were right," she said with bitterness coating it. "She didn't like a single design. You'll be happy to know—"

"You think I would be happy that all your backbreaking work came to nothing?"

She had the sense to look ashamed. *Theos*, she truly believed him to be a sadistic monster, didn't she? Had he ever given her reason to believe otherwise?

"How so?" he asked, noting the lines of strain around her mouth.

Now, she looked stunned. "What do you mean?"

"Why did she reject them? Did she give a reason?" When she still stared at him blankly, irritation touched him. "I'm trying to have a conversation, not attack you," he burst out.

"She thought they were far too high-end for her store, way too sophisticated and bohemian for the clientele that comes to her boutiques. *Too geared toward the jet-setting club like your husband's* were her exact words."

Whatever she had shown her, Mrs. Dupont had refused to budge from her stance. Disappointment settled on Leah's shoulders like a heavy cloak. Had she risked everything for nothing?

"So what is your plan of action next?"

She pulled her attention back to Stavros, sharply aware of his potent presence in her small workroom. In every conversation they had ever had about her work, his interest had been genuine, and suddenly she felt like an ungrateful bitch. Grabbing the notebook, she showed him the notes she had scribbled earlier. "I did what you said I should do in the first place. Had a lengthy discussion about her expectations." That he asked so politely made her failure even more real. "So it's back to the drawing board for me."

He took the book from her and flipped through the notes. "Didn't you leave the fashion house because you wanted to give your own vision a try?"

It had been the foremost thought in her head since Mrs. DuPont had left. "Yes, it was. But it also means walking away from a sure customer, and continuing to trust my vision."

Leaning by her side, he crossed his ankles. The long stretch of his legs in front of her, his tapering waist, the breadth of his shoulders...his masculinity was a striking contrast against her silks and dresses.

"Tell me... all the ideas you discussed today, do they excite you enough to want to risk everything like you did with me?"

Sucking in a deep breath at how effectively he shot to the heart of the matter, Leah shook her head. Talking strategy with him was the last thing she had expected.

He threw the book on the table and turned to her. "Then it is as simple as saying no, and forging ahead."

"But—"

"I saw Anna wearing that red dress and I believe that you're talented, Leah. Add to that, a rich husband who's willing to feed you and supply you with endless fabric. Trust your gut and go for it."

Stunned into a monosyllabic response, Leah stared after his retreating form hungrily, all of her crushing disappointment from the day leaving her in a whoosh. Every muscle in her body ached and yet she felt like there was a renewed fire in her.

And it was thanks to the man she had deceived and hated for years.

CHAPTER SEVEN

LEAH SMOOTHED DOWN the fabric of the beige, supremely boring satin silk she was wearing and suppressed another sigh. The dress, picked by the stylist and coming with a hefty designer tag, wasn't ugly per se.

But the classic fitting bodice and the flaring skirt were not at all her style. With her hair pulled back from her face and the cashmere wrap, she felt thoroughly unlike herself. The heavy diamond choker lay against her throat like a dead, cold weight that could siphon off every bit of warmth from her skin.

Blinking, she looked at Stavros sitting on the other side of the wide cabin, his arrogant head bent to his laptop.

She unbuckled the seatbelt and paced the length of the long cabin all the way to the rear and back.

Her back ached from all the work she had done the past few weeks, once she had received the delivery of all the raw material she had ordered.

In the evenings, she had had meetings every day of the week, some arranged by her, some by the man who, it seemed, would never relent in his duty.

She had met with a graphic designer, a contact she had made working at the fashion house, who was designing her website; a seamstress who had come in from the village because, like Anna, she had heard what Leah did and begged to work on them with her, because she loved dress-making; and with an attorney that Stavros had arranged to take care of trademarking her label and setting up a company in her name.

Tears had filled her eyes when she had eyed the paperwork with her name on it.

Leah Huntington Sporades—Head Designer.

Her father would have been so proud of her. Giannis, if he knew, would be so proud of her. Even more so, because he had started Katrakis Textiles as a small retail merchant decades ago. But seeing him would mean getting close to him and she couldn't risk that.

Stavros had stood witness to all of it, a silent specter in the room as the platinum-tipped pen had slipped from her hand a couple of times when she wanted to sign the papers. Lost in the magnitude of the moment, she had felt grateful for his hand on her shoulder.

"Have you picked a name for the label?" his question had boomeranged in the silence, testing her strength.

Calista and she had made so many plans. She had been the one who had pushed Leah into stretching her wings, given her confidence that her designs were brilliant. Had worn the dress Leah had designed to her eighteenth birthday party and had dazzled the world in it.

Holding the logo she had come up with with the help of a graphic designer—an elaborately stylish L and C tangled up together, she whispered, *"Leah & Calista."*

His silence beat down on her as she braced herself against his censure.

All her hopes and happiness tied to that name, she couldn't feign defiance. Couldn't muster any defense against his intrusion into what was a monumental moment for her. Would have crumbled into pieces if he had pushed her.

But he had said nothing. Neither praise nor judgment.

Only studied her with a strange light in his eyes until the room had swelled and collapsed around them, echoing with her lies and his questions.

The waiting lawyer had finally cleared his throat and Leah had looked away.

After that day at the pool, Stavros and she had fallen into a surprising routine. Every evening, when he returned from work, he would come into her workroom and they would discuss his business and her work like two polite strangers reading from a script, carefully steering away from any number of topics.

And the elephant in the room, that sharp and growing awareness of each other, roamed free.

At least she had made a lot of progress in the week. And by the end of the day, her back hurt, her fingers ached, and she fell into bed exhausted.

To Leah, it felt like the calm before the storm. But she was determined to continue the peace for as long as he was determined to keep her future hanging in the balance.

So when he'd walked into her workroom yesterday morning, his skin tanned in the glorious Greek sun, and declared that she needed a break after a grueling week, she had readily assented, even if the thought of going away somewhere with him filled her with all kinds of tension.

Had not even blinked when he had told her that they would be attending a small party, would be staying away for a week and that he'd arranged a stylist for her.

He had stood there, as solid and magnificent as ever in a white shirt and tight jodhpurs and riding boots, sweaty and sexy and insanely real, waiting for her to argue and throw a fit.

She had rubbed a hand over her chest, as if she could appeal to her heart to stop its frenzied clamoring. Delusional really, that she still thought she could beg, force or control her body when it came to Stavros.

Did he hate how she dressed? The stinging question had come to her finally. But she had nodded and thanked him, like the dutiful Leah he wanted her to be.

So here she was, on his private jet this time, ensconced

in sheer luxury. Thick cream carpet that swallowed her, spacious rear cabin with a huge king bed, and the man who was turning her inside out, as always.

Sighing, she locked her fingers in her lap when all she wanted was to sweep her fingers into the elaborate updo the stylist had twisted her hair into.

The weight of her thick hair piled into that unceremoniously tight knot pressed against the back of her head and neck. Tension piled into her shoulders.

When the stewardess arrived and inquired after her, she requested sparkling water and aspirin.

"You do not feel well," he stated in that final tone of his.

In a movement that was as graceful as it was quick, he reached her side of the aircraft. His seat was not attached to hers yet he was far too close.

She remained stubbornly silent, determined to win the war against herself.

"You've been fidgeting uncontrollably for the past hour."

"If I'm disturbing you, I—"

"*Theos*, Leah. For once, just answer my question."

"I… I don't like this hairstyle or this dress. They make me feel like…" Closing her eyes, she leaned back against her seat. God, she couldn't have sounded like she was ten years old if she had tried harder.

"Like what?" his tone hovered between resigned amusement and curiosity.

She took the water and aspirin from the stewardess and swallowed it while it watched her.

"Answer me, Leah."

Fighting the urge to burrow into herself like a turtle, she said, "I look like your version of me."

"My version of…" He looked stunned. "Explain."

"In this dress and jewelry, I am Leah Sporades, the demure and dutiful wife of respected billionaire Stavros Sporades. There's nothing of me in this. It is all you."

He froze and it seemed air and sound, the very matter around them froze along with him. "I do not understand."

"That stylist you hired, she—" she forced herself to breathe "—this is what she presented me with."

Frowning, he ran his gaze over the straps and over the tight ruffles of the bodice.

Her skin warmed up as if she was a flower and he was the very sun she craved. Leah tightened her fists to stop from covering herself.

He cleared his throat, his nostrils flaring. "I agree that it is not your usual...style."

She nodded, wondering why she couldn't have just shut her mouth. Why some stupid, irrational, brazen part of her always insisted on putting herself in his line of fire. Why, even as she hated his overbearing interference, she recklessly courted it.

"You are saying that this stylist, that someone in my staff picked, chose...this *demure, dutiful little outfit*," he repeated her words, "based on how I want my wife to be presented to the world?"

"Yes."

He lounged in his chair, his expression thoughtful. "Why did you give in then? You won't even breathe air if it means following my orders."

"You commanded an army to help me get dressed for a party. Like any sane person would, I assumed that you hate how I dress. Just as you hate how I breathe, talk and generally conduct my life."

"I don't hate how you dress. You do, somehow, own and wear the flimsiest articles of clothing of I have ever seen..."

"*That is* my style as a designer—light and dreamy bohemian pieces," she sputtered, affronted.

"...and will probably expire either because of the sun or the cold one of these days, but you always look sexy and sophisticated."

Little pinpricks of heat awoke all over and her gaze flew

to his. He stared right back, as if daring her to challenge his accurate and somehow intimate observation of her style. Or maybe his right to comment on it.

The moment stretched and morphed into something else, a strange heat filling the cabin.

Accepting defeat under the thundering boom of her heart, Leah looked away. She cleared her throat and fingered the fabric of her dress.

"For all my sins, *thee mou*, I did not dictate how you should be dressed."

She looked up. "Then she, like everyone else in the world, rightfully believes that you are ashamed of me and decided that her job was to make me somehow worthy of you."

"Do not push me, *yineka mou*." The glitter in his eyes pushed Leah into keeping mute. "Tell me why you relented, Leah."

She looked away, squirming under his leisurely scrutiny. "I'm being dutiful, cooperative…"

The words trailed on her lips as he started laughing.

It swelled in the decadently silent cabin, crept inside her, filling every yearning space with itself. Scraped against her senses, like a physical thing meant to incite that relentless clamoring in every cell again.

"When you laugh, you almost look human," she blurted out.

"As opposed to an alien?"

"As opposed to a man whom I've never seen to be anything but rigid, autocratic, and driven by duty and responsibility. When was the last time you did something because you wanted to do it and not because your lofty sense of morals said you should do it? Something that's totally crazy but feels unbearably good? Something that devours you until you have it?"

Lazy interest flickered in his face. Little pinpricks of

desire uncurled within her. "What and when was the last time you did something like that?"

Her throat dry, Leah licked her lips. "I ate half a cheesecake that Rosa baked for me last night. It was heavenly."

That tawny gaze fell to her mouth. And lingered. "Wanting to do something with an utter madness is usually a sign of why you shouldn't."

Leah could very well imagine that mouth, beautifully carved and yet cruel, pressing on hers, could feel the liquid desire skitter across her skin.

"Living like that, with no thought to the future or the people around has lasting effects, *pethi mou*. It's a choice that has consequences beyond one."

"Like what?"

He shrugged, something shuttering in his expression.

"How is it that Dmitri and you are such close friends and he didn't corrupt you at all?" Leah asked.

"Maybe I'm incorruptible."

The cocky rise of his brows goaded her on. "Maybe," her heart beat so loud, "the right temptation to corrupt you hasn't come along."

The challenge simmered in the air. But terrified as she was, Leah wouldn't look away. Something about that hard, unyielding arrogance of his shattered her usual defenses, drove her to one risk after the other.

Being in his company made her forget all her fears, she realized with a staggering self-awareness.

Suddenly, he caught her hands and dragged her forward on the seat. Only his hands touched hers, and yet she was aware of every inch of her skin.

"You have been working all kinds of hours this week."

"Don't sound so surprised." She searched for something to concentrate on instead of his tight clasp. "Anyway, so do you."

"Yes, but mine is not grueling, backbreaking work like yours. Rosa tells me you take frequent breaks to stretch and run, so that's good." He turned her hands around in his, as if testing the weight and fit of them against his. Slowly resting them back in her lap.

"So you do admit that I know how to take care of myself?"

"I never disagreed that you have the faculty for that. Whether you choose to use it or not…" Uncharacteristic hesitation danced in his face. "Leah, I ordered an army because I thought you would enjoy being pampered for a day. Thought you would like dressing up, have a chance to catch up with others like you. You did say my estate was in the middle of nowhere."

Warmth swelled in her chest and spilled over. Nothing she said to herself to contain it helped.

She was like the pathetically adorable little puppy that whimpered and promised forever for a little bit of attention and kindness.

Did she thank him for it or did she brazen it out with an inappropriate remark? In the end, she did neither. Just nodded and stood up, suddenly feeling caged in her own skin.

She wanted to, *needed to*, hate Stavros. And seeing this side of him was slowly but surely eroding the entire foundation of her life.

"What kind of party requires that we stay there for a week?"

"Katrakis Textiles is celebrating its fiftieth year anniversary. Tonight's grand celebration is to honor everything Giannis has accomplished in the past fifty years. And then we will spend a week with him."

Katrakis Textiles—Giannis's legacy for Dmitri, Stavros *and* her. "I want no part of it."

"I don't believe you."

Trembling with panic, Leah locked her hands by her sides, the urge to pound at him rising again.

"I'm not lying about this. Dmitri and you are welcome

to it. Now if you could please tell your pilot to turn around and head back to your estate—"

He didn't even blink. "I won't. Maybe I forgot to mention it, but this is one of the conditions you have to meet for your freedom, Leah."

Her throat felt like it was made of glass. "You can't do this."

Rising from his seat, Stavros planted himself in her way. He frowned, taking in the trembling of her shoulders, the real flare of panic in her eyes. "Leah, what's going on?"

Her chin tilted up, her gaze slowly focusing on him again. Jaw gritting, she squared her shoulders. "I don't want anything to do with Giannis or his legacy. He…rejected my mom without looking back just because she fell in love with my dad. He didn't even come when she died, he never accepted my dad."

"He was heartbroken that he had driven your mother away, Leah. And she…she was just as stubborn as him."

"He loved you and Dmitri more than he ever loved her or me. He took me in because he had no choice after my dad died."

"He tried to make amends for his mistakes."

Leah shook her head, forcing the words to come. "He did what he failed to do with my mom, to me. He…he ruined my life by bringing you into it. He took away my freedom by forcing you to marry me."

"He did not force me, Leah. I owed him everything in my life. I would have made any sacrifice he…"

She recoiled from him as if he had struck her.

Christos! She was a complex puzzle he would need to spend a lifetime to understand.

Beneath the reckless defiance, beneath her constant animosity for him, did Leah want his approval?

"Of course," she said, her voice trembling. "The great Giannis Katrakis who's made kings of his godsons, plucked them from poverty and obscurity…and the honorable Stavros Sporades who would do anything for him, to the point of marrying his obnoxious granddaughter…and whose life has been ruined by it?

Mine.

"I'm not an instrument in achieving redemption for Giannis or for you to show your gratitude."

"You don't understand how much he longs to—"

"And you do? You understand feelings and fears, Stavros? Even Calista's death…all it means to you is a failure… Do you ever miss her? Did she ever mean anything to you other than being a responsibility?"

Tight grooves appeared by his mouth, his stunning face white beneath his dark skin. He looked haunted. "I took care of her since she was a crawling toddler. I—"

"*You took care of her, you protected her, you bought her clothes and jewelry,* but did you ever love her? Does Giannis mean anything to you other than a debt to repay? Am I anything but a penance for your supposed failure? God, it's like your heart is nothing but stone."

Pure fury wreathed his features and yet, he didn't scare Leah. All she wanted was to hurt him for pushing her to this.

First her father, then Calista—they had left her shattered, inconsolable, alone. Yet, somehow she had managed, she had found something she loved and started pouring her heart and soul into it.

She couldn't risk getting attached to her grandfather, she couldn't survive another loss.

"Everything you have ever done has been self-serving, and you dare to question me?" he shot back.

"Yes, I dare. You have no fears, no doubts, nothing that holds you back from what you think is right. Don't pretend like he means something to you."

"Giannis is the father I never had. He's been a better mother to me than the one who walked out on us. He has been my family, my friend; he's everything to me. He came for me based on a small promise my drunkard father roped him into making for some age-old village tradition. If he hadn't kept his word, I wouldn't have known kindness or honor. I would have spent my life in poverty and misery. So yes, I would do anything if it means it would bring a smile to his face."

His outburst stunned Leah, the ache in those words irrefutable, rendering her bitter accusations a lie. That he had suffered neglect at the hands of his parents, that there was so much depth to his determination toward his duty, it shook her from within.

The silence rang with his fury, his movements caged and restless.

He ran a hand over his eyes and exhaled, suddenly looking extremely tired. A haunted look wreathed his features. "I don't care if you think he ruined your life. All he ever intended was to keep you safe, even from yourself.

"So you will not only act how Giannis Katrakis's granddaughter and heiress should tonight, you will also spend the next few days with him, and you will tell him how grateful you are for everything.

"If you know what's good for you, and I think that is one thing you know very well, you will obey me."

CHAPTER EIGHT

LEAH LOOKED OUT from the huge balcony that gave a view of the lush acreage surrounding her grandfather's house.

The estate was covered with huge marquees. Multicolored fountains were lit up in the grounds, buffet tables groaning under the weight of delicacies and dishes. Soft music filtered from unobtrusive speakers nearer the house.

Laughter and greetings in Greek floated up from the crowd of two hundred or more guests, piercing through the melancholy that gripped her. In the half hour or so she had spent down there, she had only heard goodwill for Giannis and praise for Stavros and Dmitri.

It seemed her grandfather couldn't have chosen better men to continue his legacy. She was the outsider, the curiosity, the unknown, and being among people who had known her mother, the fact hurt. Yet she had no one but herself to blame.

When she had stepped out of the limo on Stavros's arm, it was as if the entire world had come to a standstill. Thundering silence had reigned as she had walked through the parting crowd, her gaze both searching for and bracing for the sight of her grandfather.

He's taking a break, Stavros whispered in her ear and her breath left her in a ball. Her knees would have buckled beneath her if he hadn't held her up against his solid frame.

An hour later, here she was waiting for Giannis, everything she had done over the past decade rushing up toward her.

She hadn't been in her grandfather's house for almost eight years now, having chosen to live with Calista at Stavros's house even before he had tied her to him. The grand house was as lifeless as Stavros's house had been full of peace.

Her grandfather had been so open and loving of her when Stavros had brought her home. Just fifteen, she had been grief-stricken, too shattered by her father's sudden death to respond to Giannis with anything more than single-word responses. But he hadn't given up on her. He had bid Stavros to bring Calista along next time. And just as he had predicted, Calista had been a welcome storm in her life— fun, reckless, daring, and somehow, she had understood Leah's grief.

Except Leah had never imagined it would be Calista that she would lose.

Crippled by Calista's loss, stunned by Stavros's decision, she had refused to even look at Giannis. If she didn't love him, if she didn't hug him as her arms sometimes ached to, if she didn't pin all her love on her kind grandfather who told her thrilling tales about a mother she had never known, she wouldn't have to live through another loss.

If she didn't love him, there would be no pain when he was gone. Even when Giannis had recovered from his heart attack, she had refused to see him.

Stavros was right. She had truly become selfish. A coward who cared about nothing but protecting herself from pain.

Something broke her reverie and she turned around.

Stavros standing slightly behind him, for support she knew, her grandfather stood under the archway, his brown eyes hungrily studying her. "Come close so I can see you." His voice, soft and coarse, reverberated in the stillness.

Tugged as though by invisible cords, she took a few steps. Her heart thudded in her chest.

"You look so much more like her now, so much like my beautiful Ioanthe. Welcome home, Leah."

And just like that, every defense she had put in place, every wall she had erected around her heart, came tumbling down.

Tears overflowing onto her cheeks, half blinded by the emotion engulfing her, Leah stumbled toward him. Wrapped her arms around him with no regard to his frail body, with no thought other than to lose herself in his unconditional acceptance. On the periphery, she heard Stavros's soft curse.

Giannis was so thin and insubstantial that if not for Stavros anchoring them, she knew she would have toppled them down. "I'm so sorry," she whispered, a haunting void in her gut.

How cowardly she had been to deny herself his embrace, his love?

Her grandfather held her with a tight grip. The remembered pine scent of him made her tremble. "Shhh...do not cry, *thee mou*."

When she became aware of her surroundings again, Giannis was sitting in a chair and she was kneeling in front of him, the stone floor digging into her knees. Overwhelmed by shame and grief, she hid her face in his knees while he kept his hand over her head, whispering endearments. Even in the turmoil she was in, she knew Stavros had left them alone. Breathing loudly, she swiped her fingers over her cheeks and looked up.

"I'm a coward. All I ever cared about was protecting myself."

He shook his head and smiled, tucking her hand into his. "You are here now."

She wouldn't be if not for Stavros. But with all her old

fears swirling beneath the joy of seeing her grandfather, Leah couldn't be grateful to Stavros. Not yet.

Leah's soft cries haunted Stavros as he paced room after room, trying to find her. More than two hours had passed since he had left her with Giannis and rejoined the party, his thoughts in a whirl.

When Giannis had brought him to this very mansion years ago, it had taken him a month to learn the layout of the house. Now he cursed it.

His nurse had just informed him that Giannis had returned to his bedroom an hour ago. Which meant Leah could be anywhere.

A sense of failure haunted him, a gnawing in his gut just as in the days after Calista had died. Had he pushed her too far tonight? Why had she cried as though her heart had been breaking?

Her reaction to seeing Giannis shook Stavros on levels he couldn't grasp.

He finally found her in the dark music room, a shadow sitting in silence. Ioanthe used to play piano here, he remembered Giannis telling him fondly.

Stepping inside, he flicked the switch on and light from the overhead crystal chandelier flooded the room.

His chest swelled with a sudden surge of emotion as his gaze found her on the chaise longue, her legs tucked under her, her dress billowing around her.

"I wouldn't comment on the wine bottle, or my dress or how I live my life just now, Stavros." She flicked him a wary glance, guilty color streaking her cheeks. A bottle of red wine sat on the vanity table, a half empty glass in her hand. "I'm painfully alive, so that should be good enough for you."

His breath came out in shuddering exhale, old fear lurking just beneath the surface.

Her hair had come undone from the severe style she

hadn't liked, framing her face in disarray. Her eyes looked a little swollen and that laughing, mocking, sensuous mouth was pinched at the corners. Face scrubbed of makeup and huddled against the dark red upholstery, she looked achingly innocent, and lonely. And *afraid*, he thought frowning.

"Are you hiding from me, Leah?"

Her sigh rattled in the silence. "Would it help my case if I said I was?"

Irritation flickered inside him. Couldn't she tell him even such a tiny truth?

Even the proper, demure dress had lost its war against her. Crumpled and stained at the hem where she must have been kneeling while one strap hung half down her arm, it bared her neck and the upper swell of one breast. The diamond choker glittered against her slender throat.

A relentless peal of hunger began to simmer through him. His fingers itched to trace that delicate collarbone, his mouth tingling to press against the pulse hammering at the base of her throat.

But even as desire ran rampant in his veins, it was the underlying thread of tenderness that unsettled him. He should have been happy that she had done as he had asked, that she hadn't hurt Giannis as she had…*hurt him? Wounded him?*

You are made of stone.

How had her words found such purchase in him? Another new awareness that only Leah could elicit, another new territory that she pushed him into…

Theos, what was wrong with him?

Tucking his hands in the pockets of his trousers, he leaned against the doorway.

"You don't look like my version of you anymore. You look like…you. Even that dress…I think you have bent it to your will, Leah."

"I'm glad to hear that," she said, sounding anything but. "Aren't you done pulling my strings tonight?"

The dare in her tone would have made him smile if

he could have believed it completely. If he hadn't heard the quiver she worked hard to suppress. If he hadn't seen such ache and longing ravage her fragile face when she had seen Giannis.

Still, he played along, unsure of her mood. Even more dangerous, unsure of his own intentions. "Have you still not learned not to challenge me, Leah?"

She looked down into her drink and he had a feeling she wanted to hide from him. That she didn't want him to see her like this at all.

"I'm telling you to leave me alone, Stavros." She confirmed his suspicions. "I'm telling you that I feel as reckless and deranged as you have always called me. I'm telling you to not dissect my actions today and pronounce judgment."

Even as her tone rose, she still didn't meet his eyes.

Had he made it so hard for her to show him anything but that selfish facade? Was he truly such an unfeeling monster then?

Had he always been like that?

He had worked so hard at his grandfather's small farm, trying to pitch in for his father's negligence, afraid that they would throw Calista and him out on the streets.

He remembered a strange calm the night his grandmother had said his mother wasn't coming back; he remembered not shedding even a tear when he had found out that his father was dead. All he had thought of even that day was how he would shield Calista from it.

For as far back as he could remember, it had been about the little girl that had followed him around from the moment she had been able to walk, hugging him, kissing him, and coming to him with tears when she had a bruise, knocking the breath out of him.

She had had such trust in her eyes that he hadn't known, literally, what to do with it. Hadn't known how to return those hugs, hadn't known what he could say to her. So instead he had done what he could.

He had protected her, provided her with everything he possibly—

Theos, no!

The thought that had always brought such comfort to him now flayed him, digging in, making him flinch in pain.

Do you actually miss Calista? Did you ever love her?

Had Leah been right in her cruel judgment of his feelings for Calista too?

After he had lost Calista, he had felt angry, confused, unbalanced. His failure poisoned his very thoughts, so he shoved them away and focused on his actions instead.

Protecting Leah, and punishing himself and her, had provided him with perverse relief.

Now, her words taking root inside him, he felt raw.

He should leave her, every instinct warned him. He should walk away when all she was capable of was piercing him with her acerbic words. He should be done with her, set her free and not look back.

And yet, he couldn't have walked away if his very breath had depended on it.

Beneath his duty toward Giannis and his sense of responsibility toward her, even beneath his unnerving attraction to her, something very strange had begun to flutter in him for Leah.

He was in awe of that feeling as much as he was wary of it.

"What else do you intend to put me through in this test of yours, Stavros?"

Everything about what he had seen tonight troubled him. "Leah, was your hatred of me reason enough to keep away from Giannis?"

The wariness slowly dissipated as she held his gaze and finished her drink. Something new dawned in her glittering gaze—a satisfaction, and his breath rattled. One long leg stretching in front of her, her stance loosened. Her slender shoulders squared, her nostrils flared.

"I would let you think that if I thought it would hurt you. I would do anything right this moment if I thought it would make you bleed."

He found himself walking toward her, found himself straddling the lounger to face her. It was as though the combination of pain and fury in her eyes tugged at him.

She looked glorious, infinitely breathtaking.

She had already somehow pierced him, the truth lingered on his lips. The thought of that vulnerability, of sharing that much with her made his gut clench.

Clasping her cheek, he lifted her to face him, his pulse pounding in his veins. The sound of her sharp breath was like a balm to him. "Are you so thirsty for my blood then, *pethi mou*?"

"Yes."

Her resounding answer sent a shiver through to his very bones. It was as though seeing Giannis had peeled off that facade of hers.

"Are you satisfied, Stavros? Have I risen in my worthiness in your eyes?"

The thunderous roar of his heart, the curling heat in his muscles made it harder for him to whisper the one question that had been battering at him all day. He felt as if a huge truth was within his grasp, as if the real Leah was within his reach. And in that moment, he would do anything to have it.

To have her, to know her, to feel her...

If he had her, would the strange turmoil inside him stop?

"When has my opinion of you begun to matter, Leah?" he whispered softly, the words burning on his lips.

He felt her instant recoil in the stillness of her form, in the way the very air around her seemed to suspend and freeze.

A violent energy burst from her limbs. Lifting the hem of that heavy, voluminous dress away from her legs, she faced him. A flash of a toned thigh met his gaze and he looked away guiltily, the depth of his hunger for her shredding his control.

Her hair whipped around her face, the swish of her dress adding to the harsh exhales of her breath.

The uncaring mask back in place, she mocked him with that practiced glare in her eyes, with that biting edge to her tone. By hiding from him what he so desperately wanted to see.

"You know what, Stavros? Scratch that answer. I don't care whether I could hurt you or not. I don't give a damn about you. I did what you asked of me, I made sure Giannis is happy. I played the part of an heiress and his loving granddaughter to the hilt. Which means I'm one step closer to achieving my freedom. *That's* what I care about.

"Tell me what will make the next month go faster so that I can see the back of you. Tell me what is next so that I never have to talk to you ever again."

A dangerous fire burst in his belly.

How dare she put on this mask again? How dare she deny him even the merest hint of the real her? How dare she sink under his skin and yet deny him the same satisfaction?

How dare she turn him into this man teetering on the edge of his control, and walk away so blithely?

Before she could get to her feet and escape, because he had no doubt that she was about to escape, he clasped her wrist and tugged her down.

She fell onto her haunches, her shoulders knocking against his chest. For the first time in his life, Stavros gave in to every irrational urge, every desperate want. "What are you afraid of, Leah? Me or yourself?" he taunted.

Primal satisfaction pounded through him, the increasing frenzy of her movements telling him he had hit the mark. "I'm not afraid of you," she said, twisting her upper body to get away from him. Ended up torturing him further with the slide of her body against his.

"Then face me, Leah," he whispered, driven by some

reckless urge to prove that his opinion mattered to her, that he mattered to her.

Just as she was beginning to matter to him...

She couldn't let him touch her, she couldn't let him kiss her.

If she let him touch her tonight, if she let him hold her tonight, something inside her would break. She would pour out the whole wretched truth, she would blurt how lonely she had been...

If she let him see the real her, she would have no shield, no armor against him. And even in the fragility of her emotions, Leah knew she couldn't let Stavros close.

"Why are you acting like this?"

Her arms ached with the effort it took to hold herself so stiffly in the circle of his body; every inch of her hurt to stay unaffected in the warmth of his rough embrace.

"Like a man acts with his wife?"

She fought back stupidly hot tears, knowing that she didn't stand a chance against that claim.

When she pushed against his wrists again, he grabbed her hands this time. Laced her fingers through his and pulled her forward. Her hip touched his rock-hard thigh and she bit down on her lip.

Giving up her struggle, she leaned her forehead against his shoulder. "What do you want from me?"

"All I've ever wanted is the truth, *pethi mou*." His fingers circled her nape with a possessively delicate touch. Her heart thudded as if it would thunder out of her chest as she raised her head. Molten heat filled his eyes. "But you won't give me that. So, I will claim what I can of you."

Somehow she shook her head, even mesmerized by how low and silky he sounded, by how astonishingly expressive his face was.

How had she always seen only one facet of Stavros?

There were so many sensations—the rough texture of his hands against hers, his bruising grip on her wrists, the sudden heaviness of her breasts as they jutted against him, the beckoning hardness of his thighs against her hips—she should have expired from so much sensory input. It was as though her body was one pealing, pulsing mass of sensation...

He was everything she ever wanted and yet she couldn't give in. "I don't want this. I..."

"In this, you're not a good liar." He placed a finger on the pulse at her neck, feral satisfaction filling his gaze. "Your pulse betrays you...your darkening eyes betray you." With every word he said, his accent became thicker, her breaths came faster. "Even your mouth betrays you..." His long fingers framed her cheeks, pulling her closer.

Her hips nudged his thighs apart, and the hottest sensation zigzagged through her. His thighs were so hard and powerful, his touch possessive and potent.

How was she supposed to resist him when he looked at her like that?

"I will not be your wife soon. I won't—"

He smiled then, and the sinful curve of his mouth, the dark laughter in his eyes undid the last layer of her willpower. "Now, tonight, in this moment, you're still mine, *yineka mou.* One kiss for all the trouble you have caused me, Leah, one kiss for everything you deny me..."

He had turned her life upside down, and now he was doing the same to her heart.

Even as he staked his claim, he didn't take the kiss. Long lashes hiding his gaze, his arm around her waist a heavy weight, he paused. But sinking under a deluge of emotions, Leah stared, transfixed, at the bow shape of his leanly sculpted mouth, felt need trump every fear.

Covering the last millimeter, she pressed her mouth to his. His savage growl shocked her as much as the incinerating texture of his lips...

His mouth was hot and hard, and a million sparks exploded under her skin.

With erotic strokes, he left her no air to breathe, gave her no room to think. Sensation exploded as he slanted his lips this way and that, his fingers in her hair holding her immobile for him. Teeth bit into her lower lip and punished. When she moaned, he softly blew at the spot before nipping again.

One hand slid over her hips, moved possessively over to her buttocks and then pulled her closer until she was straddling him. But not close enough for her to feel the part of him that she wanted to...

Even that, he controlled.

Her breasts felt full and aching as he crushed her against the wall of his chest with a palm at the base of her back. She panted, her breath balling up in her throat. Trembling, she ran her fingers over her mouth, and her cheek where his stubble had scratched her skin.

That mouth that could lacerate her with words, God, it could weave such erotic magic...those hands that had dumped cold water on her, they could evoke such heat in her; the cradle of his arms, it made her feel so alive...

He didn't kiss softly, he didn't seduce, he didn't cajole.

He wrung the response out of her as he did everything else with her. Impinging his will on her senses, imprinting his hard muscles over her soft ones... The way he ruled her life, the way he decided what she needed.

She could have spent the next hundred years wedged against his hardness, lost in his kiss, delirious with the pleasure he brought her. But not let him tell her what she needed, not accept what he deigned to give her.

No!

In that, she couldn't let him decide her fate, couldn't let fear rule her.

Determined to give him a fight, determined to demand her due, she pulled her mouth away from his, trailed it along that hard jawline, buried it in the crook of his neck. Tasted the salty tang of his skin. An insistent pull began at her sex, and she moaned against his bristly jaw.

His grip loosened in her hair, his other hand loosely anchoring her against him as she caressed him roughly, learned every muscle and sinew.

She touched him everywhere, reveling in the tensile hardness of him. Traced up his rock-hard thighs, up toward his groin. And her palm found his erection—hard and long and so utterly arousing... Her breath jerked in her throat.

She had done this to Stavros. The harsh rhythm of his breath in her ears, that incredible stillness of him around her...

Goaded by a clamoring instinct, she shaped him with her palm, moved her finger down the length of him, a shiver spewing in her own muscles.

A guttural sound fell from his lips as he bucked against her hand. It lasted an infinitesimal breath but she knew he had almost surrendered then, that he had lost his rules, his very control then.

Only a second but it was still a victory.

He clasped her wrist in a vise-like grip. She looked up at him and smiled, feeling dazedly powerful, painfully glorious.

In this moment, with him...any pain would have been worth it.

Dark color filled his cheeks, his gaze haunted, agonized. "Why do you push me to the very edge, Leah?" His accent was coarse and uneven as he breathed the words into her temple. "Why do you fight me, deny me every step of the way?"

"Did you not like how I responded, Stavros?" she said shivering, and for a second, he clasped her in his warmth. If he had showed her tenderness...no, this was better. "You forced me to...to respond, just as you force me into everything. That kiss was about domination, not desire, not about taking tenderness."

He studied her, his own gaze curiously empty. "And if I had asked?" Shaking his head, he stepped away from her.

As if he didn't want her answer. When he met her gaze again, his expression was shuttered. "You're not wearing your ring."

"It's somewhere in my jewelry."

"As long as you're still bound to me, you will wear it."

She stared in stunned silence.

"It would please Giannis too. And that matters to you, doesn't it, Leah? So I don't have to worry that you would talk about our little deal with him."

"And when I'm…when I win our deal?" she forced the words out through the knot in her throat. That she would never see him again was like a lead weight in her chest.

"You will not abandon him, I know that." Retribution, if she did, rang in his tone. "And I will continue to take care of the one man who means the world to me."

Stavros left Leah without looking back, the image of her swollen mouth and dazed eyes burned into his brain forever. If he stayed another minute, he didn't know what he would do.

He was unknown to himself the way he had reached for her, the way he craved her. In that moment, he had so desperately needed to claim something of her. Shuddering with frustrated desire, he wondered if she had given him anything that he hadn't taken, wondered why it mattered so much, now.

One of these days, he would be releasing her from their marriage. He knew it as surely as the taste of her still floated on his lips.

Yet, instead of anticipating his freedom, all he suddenly knew was a keen urgency.

To understand Leah, to steal a part of her for himself even as she denied him.

CHAPTER NINE

WHY HAD HE kissed her?

The question haunted Leah endlessly.

What had driven her into giving in so easily?

If she closed her eyes, she could still hear his harsh breath, his softly spoken words...

Her fingers shook and her scissors slipped on the fabric. With a frustrated cry, Leah threw the scissors across the room and fingered the silk gently.

The sheer tulle she was cutting for the underskirt of the wedding gown was the most expensive fabric that she had ordered for her collection. At least, the amount of cloth she had ruined was minimal.

Carefully, she folded the fabric and tucked the tissue wrapping around it. She wasn't going to get anything that needed focus done today.

More than a week had passed since the night of the party. The next evening, Stavros had left. She had had a feeling he had left because of the kiss.

There was something new—an intensity to his gaze now when he looked at her.

Walking to the rack, she took a cocktail dress in deep red. Threading the needle, she sat down on the couch and began piping the hem.

She was glad she had persuaded Stavros to have most of her materials packed and sent to her grandfather's estate. Her grandfather tired easily and without her work to keep her busy, she would have driven herself mad thinking of Stavros the whole time.

The sheer arrogance of the man, the clinical coldness with which he had made her respond—she had whimpered like a dog, for God's sake... Even that couldn't stop her from trembling every time she remembered the feel of his rough mouth, the bite of his teeth into her lower lip, the way his large hands skimmed and molded her body...

It had been her first kiss and it had been an exercise in... What? A war of wills? A balm to his ego? Or had he been as powerless as her?

Frustration carved through her.

She wanted to hate him, she did hate him for that cold resolve...but he also made her feel so alive. Lost in his kiss, drowning in his arms, there had been no place for fear, no place for hiding.

Nothing but living...

When he looked at her with such glittering desire in his tawny eyes, when he looked at her as if she could unlock something inside him...it was so easy to believe that he saw her as an equal.

Which was the stupidest thing ever given that he was with his lover in Athens attending a charity event right now... He was probably back in her bed too, she thought nastily and gasped as she pricked her finger with the needle.

The good thing was how much work she had gotten done and the time she had spent with Giannis.

After an excruciating couple of days, Giannis had finally taken pity on her and asked her to show him a dress from her collection. He had pronounced her dress beautiful and her, an extremely talented designer who would take the fashion industry by storm. Making dresses was in their blood, he had said with pride. While his praise had been extravagantly effusive, it had still filled her with warmth.

So every day, she took breakfast and lunch with him, then accompanied him on a short walk around the house.

Sometimes, they played a board game that he taught her, and sometimes, they discussed her designs. They carefully kept away from talking about Stavros and the state of her marriage.

After being afraid for so long, after training herself to not get attached to him, forming such a strong emotional bond should have been hard to do in just a few days. But spending one of those yawningly long Greek afternoons chatting with Giannis, or just sitting together in comfortable silence, or the times he would nap and she would sit with her sketchpad on the back terrace, had become incredibly precious to her.

Her grandfather was irreverent, naughty, and kind.

As the sweltering days gave way to cooler nights, her fears melted away and like the leaves slowly changing color, an incredible sense of joy pervaded her. It was so alien that she had taken to staring at herself in the mirror, wondering if it made her look different.

As her cell phone chirped, she realized it was time for lunch with Giannis.

The time that Stavros had stipulated she spend with Giannis was rapidly coming to an end, and suddenly, saying goodbye to her grandfather, even temporarily, was the last thing Leah wanted to do.

Stavros was avoiding her, she knew as surely as her heart thumped when he called every evening and asked about Giannis.

Something had changed between them that night, whether for good or bad, she didn't know.

Her footsteps clicking on the outer courtyard, Leah sighed. She could hate him all she wanted for forcing her to this, but she wouldn't have had this wonderful week with Giannis if not for him.

Leah joined Giannis at the table laid out on the back patio that offered an unending view of the shoreline. The raised porch provided shade from the Greek sun. Reaching Giannis, she kissed his papery cheek and sat down.

The small table groaned under the weight of a colorful and mouthwatering array of dishes. "I didn't know that we were having a feast today," she said, spreading her napkin on her lap. "I would have skipped breakfast and run a few more miles."

"Eat," Giannis said. "No man likes his woman so thin that it could hurt him if he embraces her."

Popping a piece of a juicy, thick-crusted pie into her mouth, Leah shook her head. "Since no man is actually intent on embracing or otherwise expressing love for your granddaughter," she continued in that same irreverent tone, "no worries there."

It had become a bit of a game this past week between them, about who could say the most outrageous thing. The smile disappeared from Giannis's face. "He is your husband, child. Are you denying him rights?"

Leah coughed, choking on the flaky piece of pastry. Recovering, she took a sip of frosty lemonade. "I don't want to ruin the afternoon by talking about it."

"Your mother is gone. Calista is gone. I learn from Stavros that you keep to yourself. Maybe talking to an old man will help, *ne*?"

His overtly sweet tone made her smile. "I do not want to talk about his rights, or how subservient I have to be because I'm his wife, grandfather."

"You want a modern marriage. I understand. But I have concern for you. You are very lonely. I see it in your eyes."

She was lonely, she had been for so many years now. That's why she had capitulated so easily to Stavros's touch.

She could almost fool herself into believing that.

"Leah?"

Leah didn't have the heart to push his concern away. It was so strange that she couldn't be angry with Giannis when he was the one who gave Stavros all the power over her, yet she could hold a grudge against Stavros himself.

Somewhere along the line, it had become a shield, she realized. A shield that was slowly beginning to get holes. That's what had changed.

Her grandfather clutched her fingers and she returned the pressure, feeling a sudden thickness in her throat.

"What Stavros and I have…it's too complicated. How can I think of him as my husband or anything else respectful for that matter if he continues to treat me like a child?"

"It is his nature to protect the people he considers close."

I'm not close to him, the juvenile taunt rose to her lips. She didn't care that she wasn't, she decided resolutely.

"I have a feeling that's all he knows how to do. He…I have never seen him laugh, never need anyone. Never seen him vulnerable." And yet, he had looked so different that night they kissed, almost vulnerable…to her touch, to her words even. "He was probably born fully formed with a set of rules about how life should be lived, in his hand."

Something flickered in Giannis's gaze and Leah swallowed the rest of her words. "Stavros does not ask, or take anything for himself. Only gives."

There was such truth in her grandfather's words that Leah stilled. She had never seen him ask, or demand anything for himself. It had only ever been about her, or Calista or Giannis, or even Dmitri sometimes. But never about himself.

Still grappling with that, she made her voice casual and gripey again. "For all I know, he does not need anything like normal people do. He will probably order the cook to not serve me if he learned I eat my dessert first."

A twinkle appeared in Giannis's eyes. "You speak like this to him?"

When she nodded, he laughed, the flimsy sound bursting out of him. It shook his frail frame, and alarm crashed through her. Sensing her anxiety, he sobered. "Laughing with you is good for me. I still believe in the rightness of your marriage. You are precisely what Stavros needs in his life. And you—" something too close to the truth lingered in his eyes "—him. I wish you would give it a real try. You will find him to be an honorable man."

Beneath his rigidness, beneath his tunnel view of the world, she hated to admit, Stavros's actions had always been driven by good intentions.

What would it be like to trust him with her fears? What would it be like to give herself over to him? To really give their relationship a try? To be the woman he shared himself with?

Feigning a nonchalance she was far from feeling, she looked at Giannis, who watched her curiously. She had seen the questions in his eyes, had seen him hesitate. And suddenly, she couldn't bear to go away with Giannis not knowing the truth.

Abandoning her food, she clasped his hand. "I didn't take drugs that night. I have never touched that stuff in my life. I know I have pained you but I…"

A catch in her throat, she pinned her forehead to his hand.

How could she put her irrational fear into words?

The sound of a soft tread, the way her skin prickled, she instantly knew.

Without turning, she let go of Giannis's hand and leaned back in her seat.

Stavros was back.

He believed her.

The realization stopped Stavros in his tracks. As powerful as the sun beating down on him, as simple as the feeling in his gut.

Just as she would never have gone to the media with her story, would never have dragged Giannis and him into a dirty scandal to facilitate a divorce.

She had been bluffing that day.

And he had fallen for it.

He had believed every lie Leah had ever told him, had spun his own theory of how she had led Calista astray, that, somehow, she had convinced his naive sister to try something dangerous...

But if Leah hadn't been the one that had pushed Calista to it, then what had happened? That Leah had lived while Calista had died of a drug overdose that night, he had chalked it up to pure chance.

But it wasn't.

Whatever choice she had made that night, his sister had made it of her own accord.

His head pounded with the questions it let loose; his entire world tilted.

Had he not really known Calista either?

"Come, Stavros," Giannis beckoned him with a smile before he could disappear with his shifting thoughts.

Stavros looked up, zeroing in on Leah with a stinging hunger.

On her way to the other side of the table, she stilled without looking at him. Her fingers slipped on the serving spoon, the sound clanging in the patio.

Slowly, she moved her head and met his gaze. The impact of it rocked through him, the picture she presented ripping through the semblance of control he had fooled himself into achieving over the past four days.

An off-shoulder, black, cutoff blouse showed a strip of her back, indented by the line of her spine, an outlandish article of clothing if he had ever seen one, and yet it suited her to perfection, with the long, gray skirt that billowed around her legs.

A soft breeze pushed it against her legs, outlining the lean, toned length of them.

Heat thrummed in every pore, his arousal painfully instantaneous.

He wanted to see if she was just as silky everywhere, he wanted to see that glorious hair, right now piled atop her head and falling from it, spread against his pillows, he wanted to feel that mouth against every inch of him...

Leah affected him like no other woman ever did, or could. Whether it was because she was his wife or because she was inherently Leah—beautiful, demanding, lively— he wouldn't know.

All he knew was that she was destroying every assumption he had made of her, inching toward her goal, once again, changing his life irrevocably.

But he couldn't let her go, not until he knew the truth about Calista. Not until he knew everything there was to know about Leah.

Not until he had tasted that luscious mouth one more time.

Just this once, he would reach for what he wanted, he would take what he craved and damn his sense of duty.

The strangest expression glittered in Stavros's eyes. Her gaze followed the corded length of his thighs as he chose the chair wedged against hers. The memory of how hard and welcoming he had been beneath her suffused her face with warmth. Hoping they would think it was the sun, she smiled pleasantly for Giannis's benefit.

Giannis slowly got up from his chair, and both Stavros and she rose from theirs. Grabbing his walking stick, he waved them off. "It is time for me to rest. You both sit," he said with such a teasing twinkle in his eyes that Leah sighed like a deflated balloon.

How would Giannis face it when Stavros finally set her free? Would Stavros tell him?

The moment Giannis was out of sight, she stood up too, the very joy she had found this morning evaporating under her own conflicting emotions.

His fingers clamping her wrist, Stavros looked up. "Stay, Leah...*please*."

The edgy request warned her not to argue.

Increasingly aware of the high-pitched chirp of a bird in the olive groves, the rustle of leaves, and the painful thud of her own heart, she studied him under the guise of bravely facing him.

As always, he was dressed in formal clothes but the shirt was unbuttoned, and his hair looked like he had messed it up quite a bit.

From the arch of his eyebrows to the straight line of his nose, from the way his mouth tilted up on one side when he smiled to the blunt nails of his long fingers, he was painfully familiar to her now...a desperate longing awoke in her, to trace that austere face, to taste him in tenderness, to just once meet him as his equal without lies and fears.

"How is your collection coming along?"

Blinking, she searched for an answer. "Very well. I finalized the design on the last dress. I'm terrified that it might not be as breathtaking as I think it is."

"The wedding gown?"

The smile came naturally then. "Yes. I have to do the cutting on it. I've been taking the fabric, laying it all out and then just staring at it for hours... I can't afford to..."

"You're nervous?" he said with such genuine warmth that she flushed.

"It's the prize of my collection but it means so much more to me. A wedding dress, as much as it has become a symbol of status and wealth and showing off in these days, it means a lot to a woman, right? It's the one day she gets to be what she longs to be all her life."

Somehow, he had moved closer to her. Her hand lay in his loosely, the pad of his thumb tracing the top of it gently. "What is that?"

"Beautiful, special, loved." Pulling her hand away from him, she smiled to herself. "No matter what age, that day, she is the center of the whole universe for this one man… that day, it's a new beginning, a fresh start, a promise she cherishes that her life will hold meaning to someone else. It's the first day of a whole new way of life, of the most important, intimate relationship she's ever going to have… and the wedding dress… it symbolizes all those hopes and dreams she's ever cherished."

Sensing his stillness, she turned and saw the lacerating pity in his eyes.

It was like the most vulnerable part of her, the part she even hid from herself, had been ripped open.

Shutting her eyes to stop the heat building behind, she saw what he remembered.

She had married in a ghastly cream silk dress that had been too tight on her chubby body. With a stone-faced Dmitri as witness while Giannis lay in a hospital bed. Drowning in guilt over Calista, numb that she always seemed to be saying goodbye to loved ones, terrified about what Stavros intended, and hating herself…

That bleary day had been about punishment and penance, about duty and fear. Just as the moment after when he had pressed his mouth to hers, had been.

Even then she had been eager for his kiss, had clung to him in her shame when he had put her away from him, and wiped his mouth.

"At least, that's the statement I want this collection to make, you know." Her blasted voice wouldn't stop quivering. "Like you said, it's a career saturated with so many fresh faces that you can disappear in a second… You have to be able to put a new spin on your collection, present it almost like a story so that your consumers will fall in love with it, and that's how—"

Clasping her chin, he turned her toward him. From casual to a vehement intensity, his expression changed in mere seconds. "Don't, *agape mou*."

Still, she tried to pretend. "You probably find this intensely boring."

"Do I not deserve the truth even in this, Leah?" Resting on his haunches in front of her seat, he took her hand in his. The tenderness in his gaze unraveled her defenses. "Do not lie about something that is so important to you, do not cheapen what truly comes from your heart. Not this…"

"I…"

"Did you once dream like this too? Was marriage that important to you?"

Her throat raw, she nodded. "I believed in the sanctity of it once, yes. My father…I never knew my mother and I always used to get this sense that a part of him was gone with her. He loved me but his heart…it was with her. When you grow up seeing love like that, you believe in its power. You start hoping for it even when you know…" She shrugged, loath to betray herself even more.

"I'm sorry for ruining your dreams, Leah," he said with such withdrawal, that it was Leah who held onto him this time. "You were a dangerous combination of recklessness and… I had to protect you from fortune hunters and—"

"Myself, of course." But there was no real bite to her words.

She could not lie and absolve him of any of it. Despite wanting to hate him, she even understood why he had done it, but his apology touched something inside her. "I wanted a lot of things. But life happened. I'll be fine, Stavros."

He nodded and rose to his feet. "What will your collection be called?"

"New beginnings."

"I do not know about dresses…" he said with such a straight face that she laughed, "but the passion I hear in your words, I am sure it will come through in what you do, *ne*?"

"You think so?"

"I believe that it will."

He said it with such confidence that a snippet of conversation she had heard between him and Giannis came back to her. Her grandfather had been asking Stavros about his contacts with major design houses and Stavros had been patiently explaining who would be open to launching a new label with a fresh designer.

Pushing her chair back, she stood up, her stomach in knots. "Your belief in me is encouraging, but I can't forever be ensconced safely in this world that Giannis and you have created for me. I can't let you and him launch a label for me using your contacts and the might of…

"If you meant your apology, if anything has changed in how you see me—" she could feel heat rising in her cheeks, but she continued stubbornly "—you'll stop arranging my life in cahoots with him."

"He wants to do it for you because he cares—"

"Becoming successful because I'm the Katrakis heiress or Stavros Sporades's wife will forever ruin my joy in this. Will you do that to me again, Stavros?

"Please… allow me the freedom to succeed or fail on my own merit. Tell Giannis to stop with this launching my label nonsense."

"If you haven't realized it, your grandfather has a will of iron—"

"And you can convince him that you could walk on water, so get him to back off."

Smiling, he nodded. "Anything else?"

She hesitated, which in itself, held Stavros's attention instantly.

"After that imperious command, what can be so hard, Leah?"

"I have been researching various fashion events and programs around the world and there's one in Athens tomorrow night that caught my attention."

"Ahhh…that's why the uncharacteristic call to my office."

She let his comment pass. "It's like a co-op event, to

be exact, an incubator for fashion design. No big labels or famous designers. Instead your... *Helene* and a group of fashion icons like her provide a stage for up-and-coming designers to showcase their talents. My application is ready. But I..."

He waited patiently.

"The entry fee is pretty hefty. Even with that, anyone who gets picked has to actually come with a recommendation from one of the event coordinators."

Wariness and pity filled his eyes and Leah blanched at it. "Helene is one of those rare women who won't take you on to do me a favor, Leah. In fact, recommending you to her will only lessen your worth in her eyes."

She shook her head, wondering if he would always think her less than capable, less than what she was. Did she have anyone but herself to blame if he did?

And why, in God's name, did the thought hurt so much?

"No, all I want is an introduction to her. My collection, at that point, will hopefully speak for me and garner her recommendation. Even if she doesn't like it, I will still get some exposure to the industry folks." Even as she confidently made her case, another tension filled her.

Just admitting the fact that Helene knew Stavros in a way Leah never would, made her want to throw up.

How could he mention the other woman so glibly? Where was his honor now, she wanted to demand. But to ask would be to show that she cared. That she spent entire afternoons wondering how he justified breaking his vows to her so boldly.

Was she so completely and irrevocably only a responsibility that he didn't think he was cheating on her?

Standing up from his chair, he extended a hand to her. "I'm sure I can convince her to give us ten minutes before the show begins." He stood tall and broad and incredibly handsome in front of her. His gaze was on her mouth; he was thinking about their kiss, she knew. Because it was impossible not to think about it. "But I need something from you in return, Leah."

The soft intonation of her name stole her breath.

He had changed toward her if he was asking and not commanding. And whatever the reason, he was even more irresistible and dangerous now.

The judging, dominating Stavros, she could hate. This insightful, approachable Stavros…she didn't stand a chance.

Spending a few days with Giannis and amassing a lifetime of memories was one thing. But tangling with Stavros, who would demand everything she had to give and more, who would bare her body and soul…she couldn't risk the pain of knowing him and then losing him.

"What," she finally managed.

"I will ask you some questions before the event. If I get a truthful answer, I will introduce you to Helene."

"Anything else I can do instead?" The moment the words were out of her mouth, she wanted to snatch them back.

He only stared at her with that intensity again. "If you won't tell me the truth, then how about a kiss?"

"You've already proved that I…I can't resist you. There is no reason for you to kiss me anymore."

He pushed a stray tendril of hair back from her forehead. And she stood very still in the wake of sensations that small touch aroused. "There is a reason."

"What?"

"That I wish to. It is only when I kiss you that I know you, Leah."

Warmth pooled in her belly, every word out of his sensuous mouth a caress and a promise. "What happened to that phenomenal willpower of yours that had the rest of us quaking in our boots?"

Laughter—hearty, gorgeous, and spine-tingling, enveloped her. "In this case, I have decided not to employ it.

"You can see Helene, Leah, but you shall have to give me your truths or your kisses. The choice is yours."

How very neatly he had trapped her, how very stupid she had been in challenging fate when she had said Stavros knew nothing but duty. His words now were honeyed, so damn seductive that her heart thudded. "What if I asked you questions?"

"But I have never lied to you. However, if you ask me a question and I do not tell the truth, you are free to kiss me, as much as you want to."

"Thanks but no thanks," Leah managed to say, past the whooshing of her heart.

Turning away from him, she ran back to the sanctuary of her workroom, wondering what had suddenly unleashed this facet of Stavros.

Her wedding gown wasn't done, but she had three other dresses she could take with her for tomorrow. Swiftly, she removed the dresses from their plastic bags and looked them over for anything to fix.

Countless hours later, she wrapped them back in the hanging bags and zipped them up.

Her heart thudded as she pulled another dress, a dress she had made for herself almost a year ago. The design had literally begged to be borne onto paper, and she had finished it in less than a week.

It was simply cut yet daring, a dress that would say all the right things about its designer. In the end, she decided to brave it out and wear it tomorrow night.

Brave because tomorrow night was going to be dangerous in so many ways that she wanted to turn the time back to a couple of months ago when it had been just her and the apartment and her blistering hatred of him...

Whatever truth he was hunting, it wouldn't be anything she'd want to tell. Which left her to face his kisses...

Running a comb through her messy hair, Leah stilled. A glimmering energy in her gaze, her pulse beating with a frenzied clamor, she looked like a stranger.

She looked almost happy.

CHAPTER TEN

HE WAS GOING to lose in his own game, Stavros decided
ruefully as Leah walked down the steps of the house the
next evening.

A game the likes of which he had never before thought of.

He was still amazed at how easily Leah made him laugh,
tease, even think of absurd scenarios just for a chance to
touch her.

Thin, almost flimsy straps at her shoulders held up the
black dress. The hem of the dress, startlingly white, ended
high above her knees in the front but fell to her ankles at
the back.

Animal-print pumps showed toned calves when she
walked down the steps.

All in all, the dress was simply elegant. Or so he thought
until she moved, waiting against his Maserati.

A flash of creamy thigh greeted his greedy gaze. The
clinging material outlined her braless breasts when she
took another step. A sudden breeze highlighted the tips of
her nipples as she neared him.

Pure, liquid lust hit him hard, and every muscle in his
body tightened, readying for pleasure.

Begging, at this point, if he was honest.

Smoky shadow and dark red lipstick turned her face
from pretty to siren... Thick glorious waves framed her
fragile features... Her cheeks were pinkened by the time
she stood in front of him...

Was that his perusal that had done this to her? Would she tell the truth when he asked or would she prefer to be kissed?

Cristos, he would never even want truth this way. All he would want was to kiss her again and again.

Because he didn't know what was the right step anymore. He didn't know where his duty ended and his need for her began...he didn't know if he was making reparations for the mistake he had made or if he just wanted to see her smile for his own selfish reasons...

For the first time in his life, Stavros was lost, didn't care about right or wrong. Only how startlingly alive he felt when he was with Leah.

"Hey," she said, reaching him.

He nodded, still absorbing the effect of her smile. She looked excited, almost happy, and he felt like he had done something right for the first time in so long.

She pointed to the top of the stairs. "So I packed up some of my collection...will you help bring it to the car?"

Inordinately pleased that she was flustered at seeing him, he halted her with a hand on her arm. "You look gorgeous."

She blinked, and then looked at him almost shyly. "Thanks, it's one of my own designs."

"It's insubstantial, sophisticated and outrageously sexy. I figured out that much."

By the time they had arrived at the venue, Leah couldn't sit still, much less think straight. And the pleasant conversation with Stavros, the way his gaze lingered over her mouth for a fraction of a second longer every time she turned toward him, it was like she was being pumped with a bit of electricity.

The powerful Maserati crawled to a stop at a centuries-old hotel and a uniformed valet immediately ran up to them.

The locks turned on with a click on the doors. Frowning, she turned toward him. "What is it?"

"Time for my first question, *pethi mou*."

"What...now?" The intensity in his expression sent tingles up and down her body. "Stavros, I'm going to show my collection to a group of intimidating professionals who make or break designers on a whim. This is not the time for some silly game that I lose whichever way—"

"Why? Do you have so much to hide?"

That shut her up promptly. "Fine," she said, bracing herself for a lacerating question.

"My estate, what did you truly think of it?"

"Austere and isolated, like you." The lie was so automatic, so swift that only after hearing it in the lush interior of the powerful vehicle did she realize that she had said it.

His gaze instantly fell to her mouth. "Liar."

In a movement that was like slow motion, he wrapped his hand around her nape and slanted his lips over hers. The gear shift dug into her side, her torso was twisted to the side, but the hot taste of Stavros's mouth...it numbed her to everything else but him.

There was no soft seduction in this kiss, no gentle erosion of her senses. No intent to dominate or control...only to take pleasure...

He pressed and licked, sucked and stroked, made love to her mouth with such raw passion that Leah couldn't breathe.

Gasping for breath, moaning in the back of her throat, she wrapped her fingers around his nape. A blistering heat spread through her, pooling at her sex as his large hand caressed her knee, climbing up her thigh...

His mouth trailed wet heat over her jaw. Sucked at the pulse at her neck. An arrow of sensation went straight to her sex and she squirmed in frustration. "God, please..."

Those devilish lips opened against her skin and she

felt his smile. "I would like nothing but to continue, *gaelika mou...*"

Her forehead flopped against his shoulders, her lungs burning for breath. "Fine, I lied. I...love that estate. It's the most beautiful, most peaceful place I have ever seen in the world. Even Giannis's estate cannot compare against such simple, stark beauty."

His silence reverberated in the interior, the remnants of lust making the tawny irises wide. "Now I wish I had shown you my bedroom."

Their gazes collided and Leah shifted in her seat, unbearable to be in her own skin. The rub of her thighs when she crossed her legs, the rasp of her dress against her nipples, every inch of her sparked with awareness. It was like the powerful car they were sitting in. She was all revved up by that kiss and yet, there was no relief.

All evening, this was what he was going to do to her. No wonder he had looked so damn interested in taking her.

How, despite all her efforts to the contrary, was it that Stavros always ended up with all the power? "You're enjoying torturing me like this, aren't you?" she whispered.

The locks on the door opened with a click. "It's very little compared to the torture you put me through all these years, *pethi mou*."

Having nothing suitable to contest that with, Leah stepped out of the car on legs that could barely hold her up.

Her dress bags draped over his shoulder casually, Stavros caught her. "Smile, Leah. The world's not going to know what's hit them when they see your creations."

With her hand over his arm, she stopped him. There was nothing but sincerity in his expression. "I would not jest over something that is so important to you, Leah."

No, he wouldn't, she realized. Whatever he decided her fate to be in the end, she would always have his support in this too.

God, how had she always been the one with such tunnel vision? How easily she had chosen to hate him, had chosen to see only the surface of him?

"How can you be so sure that I will succeed?"

"All these years, you have hidden so many things from me, and even from yourself, maybe? But when I enter your workroom, I feel all your energy, your passion. I see all of you, Leah. Such pure passion—" his gaze flicked to her mouth "—people can't help but fall in love with it."

Throwing her arms around him, Leah kissed his cheek on an impulse. The fact that a man of such willpower and discipline as Stavros believed in her dream just made her day perfect. That a man like him belonged to her, at least for tonight, it made her blood pound.

Stavros handed over Leah to Helene and accepted a glass of champagne from a waiter. The expression on Leah's face when they had entered the huge, buzzing auditorium, her exclamations as she noticed and pointed out one fashion icon after another, it had been a delight to see.

The soft touch of her lips on his cheek, he could still feel it. Her mouth had been such heaven under his and knowing that all he had to do was push his hands under that hem, that he could bare her and feast his eyes on her…it had taken him everything to bite down the urge to make love to her right there in the car.

The banquet hall where they were serving pre-show drinks and hors d'oeuvres was overflowing with designers and actresses and fashion icons, one more gorgeous than the next. And yet it was Leah his gaze followed hungrily as she flitted through the long hall, her dress sinuously draping her lithe curves.

After a while, he walked through the crowd, found her and introduced her to some more people he knew. A bittersweet feeling filled him as she introduced herself as Leah Huntington with a wary glance at him.

But, whatever his own seesawing feelings when it came

to her, he found he couldn't begrudge her the need to be herself, tonight of all times.

She returned to his side in the auditorium a quarter of an hour before the runway show was about to begin.

Her brown eyes glittered with a joy he had rarely, if ever, seen. "Now that it's too late, I'm so beginning to see the benefits of being your wife." Her words were rushed, falling over each other. "Damn, you have some pull, man."

He was as committed to his vows as he had ever been, if not more. He arrested the words, remembering how hurt she had been when he had mocked their marriage once.

And that he was utterly serious didn't bear thinking about.

He grabbed a plate from a passing waiter. "Would you like to eat something?"

She didn't wait for his reply. Reaching him, she grabbed his hand and directed the little flaky pastry into her mouth. Licked the tips of his fingers, her pink mouth closing around one. Lust hit him so quickly that he was achingly hard within seconds.

It was like a haze fell over his senses and all he could see, all he could hear was Leah. Grabbing her wrist, he pulled her behind a long column. Took her mouth in a feral kiss. Cupped her breast, covering her possessively as he had wanted to do all evening.

The rasp of her rigid nipple against his palm made him growl in the back of his throat. He dug his teeth into her lower lip. Her whimper of pain even as she clung to him stopped him. Breathing raggedly, he wondered how easily she undid him.

She glared at him. "You didn't ask a question."

He smiled, her confusion making her even lovelier. "Do not lick a man's fingers, sucking them into your mouth and then expect rationality, Leah."

Cristo, what was he doing with her?

He would, he *could* stop at a kiss, he had thought when he had come up with this game. Now, he didn't know anymore.

"Oh…" she licked her swollen mouth, and the innocent gesture sent his blood flowing south. "I will remember that when I'm tempted to lick a man's fingers next time."

The molten fury that flashed in his gaze before he willed it away made Leah want to scream in joy.

He didn't have all the power. They both had it over each other, she slowly realized.

There was something between them that denied rational explanation, that devoured self-control.

"I'll ask the question now."

Brows raised, he nodded. "Ask soon, or you will miss the show."

The simply elegant Helene's polite face had stayed with her. His friend or lover or whatever the hell she was, the woman hadn't betrayed surprise or shock or any emotion even by the flicker of a perfectly drawn eyebrow. Had talked to Leah as if it was any other fashion designer trying to break into the industry.

His kiss still stinging her lips, her will pretty much nonexistent, falling into bed with Stavros was like a fate rushing at her like an express train. If he hadn't stopped any of the times, if he willed it, she couldn't resist him, she knew.

And she refused to let him make all the rules.

"How do you…how does this work with you kissing me like this and with Helene? Are you guys taking a breather while you sort me out? What happens if you decide you want to…?"

"Yes?"

Her meager grasp on her own emotions slipping bit by bit, she shivered. Damn it, she had been so happy today and she knew it was largely because it featured him. "Don't make me say it, Stavros."

"Say it, Leah."

"Does she not mind if you…if you have sex with me?"

"Do you want to, Leah…have sex with me?"

Her spine tingled at just hearing that. "That's not the point."

"Then isn't the question moot, too?"

Frustration pumping through her, she pushed into his space. "You promised me truth, Stavros. If something happens between us before I leave, if…will you make one set of rules for me and a different set for yourself?"

His hands climbed up over her back, cradling her against him. "You hide from your own truth every day, Leah… Can you handle mine?"

"Yes."

"I told you that day aboard Dmitri's yacht that I meant my wedding vows. I have never broken them. I have not touched Helene or another woman since I married you. And I won't. Not as long as I wear your ring, as long as I'm your husband."

Her ring, her husband…

Her grip slacking, Leah fell back, and would have hit the ground if he hadn't caught her. The entire axis of her life shook, shifted and she could do nothing to stop it. "You're lying, you have to be…"

His silence jarred against her nerves.

Stavros never lied. Stavros always kept his word. Stavros lived by a code of duty and honor that was everything to him.

And she…she didn't want to lose her will to a man like that. She didn't want to be measured against him and fall short. Because, her fear would always trump everything else about her.

"It has been five years, Stavros. No man can—"

There was no nuance in his expression. "But I'm not any man, Leah." He didn't proclaim it like an achievement, he didn't dismiss it like it hadn't cost him anything. He stated it like a foregone fact.

"My word to Giannis means something to me. My vows to you mean something to me. It's true that I neglected you, did not treat you like a wife, but our marriage, it was a commitment I made intending to keep. So I waited. I waited for you to grow up. I waited for you to change. I thought I had to…"

"Fix me to be worthy of you?" she said, anger coming to her defense.

"No, I thought I should give us both time…" Something gripped his features and Leah knew that he knew it. "But then you didn't need to be changed, *ne*?"

So many years, she had wished she had had the courage to tell him the truth. That he would, for one second, see the real her. And yet now that he did, she felt naked, terrified.

The sudden silence in the long hall made her heart thud so much louder in her ears. The show had begun.

"I'll miss the show," she said, moving away. But he pulled her back. Trapped her between the pillar and his body.

"Tell me about Calista."

Her gaze flew to him. "Stavros, I—"

His hand under her chin tilted her up. "I deserve to know the truth, Leah. If you have never used drugs, that means you didn't introduce her to them."

She closed her eyes, holding back tears. "No." His silence drove her to open them again. "I went to every party you forbade me from, I drank even though most of the time I couldn't even keep it in, I flirted with boys who didn't care an iota about me because it would enrage you, I spent money only because you said not to, but I…I never touched drugs. I didn't even know that crowd…" She stopped, once again, skating the line of lies. "I didn't know where she even got it…God, if I had…"

The confusion, the guilt in Leah's eyes far too real, Stavros didn't need to ask her why she had never told him the truth before.

Because he wouldn't have believed it. He had been so blind, he had been in so much pain that he had shut everyone out. Only his failure had mattered, not the why of it.

He had so conveniently blamed Leah for it, absolving Calista of any fault.

"Then why do you carry such guilt in your eyes?"

"Because I loaned her that money a couple of days before. I was so angry with you for cutting my trip to New York short. I...hated you so much. So when she said that she needed cash, that you would never agree to give her so much, I gave her every last penny."

She flopped against him, her body shaking. Feeling as if there was an anvil on his chest, Stavros wrapped his hands around her.

Calista had borrowed it from Leah, knowing that he would not like it, probably even aware that he would take it out on Leah. *What had she been thinking?*

He hadn't known his sister then. It hung like a boulder around his neck, choking his breath. Leah had been right in this too.

Leah couldn't speak for the pain in Stavros's gaze, in his sudden withdrawal.

She had hated Stavros for being so tough on her and Calista, but Calista hadn't once mentioned her unhappiness or her problems to him.

With him, Calista had almost been a different person. Loving, smiling, obedient...as if she had just slipped into a different skin.

Now she wished she had gone to Stavros and blurted it all out.

Calista had been troubled, she realized that now. Maybe even depressed.

With hindsight, she wondered how much of that had fueled her own antagonism toward Stavros, because it had been so scary and powerless to see Calista like that. She had been mired in her own pain about her dad's death and Stavros had been a convenient target to lash out at. And yet she hated having to tell the truth now, hated this power that she had over him.

She didn't want to cause Stavros any pain.

He was rigid, he was stubborn and arrogant, but God, he had loved Calista in his own way. He had tried so hard to keep Leah away from her because he had thought her a bad influence on her. He had given Calista everything except…except listening to her.

But how could she tell him that now? How could she tell him that Calista had already been in trouble long before Leah had come into her life? That Leah had followed Calista's lead always?

The man she knew now, he still dominated, even used her attraction but hadn't she pushed him to it by dangling the truth in bits and pieces?

Calista was gone. There was nothing to be done now. There was nothing to be achieved by digging into the ugly truth.

So, she swallowed all the other truths back, bolstered her own courage and looked into his eyes.

Managing a smile, she squeezed his hand. "She was not unhappy, Stavros. I think, just restless. She…she definitely hated your rules as much as I did." She forced a smile to take the bite out of it. "But she…loved you."

He remained silent. And Leah wondered if he knew that she was quaking inside. When she had lied to him before, it had been to protect herself. This time, it was to protect him.

"I think that night whatever she took…it must have been a one-time thing. Something she thought she would try and then walk away. I'm so sorry that I gave her that money."

"You were barely nineteen, Leah. And I…made it so hard to come to me with anything, *ne*? I found fault with you at every turn, I curbed all your freedom, and then I—"

"Why?" The question barreled out of Leah.

By his actions toward her, his efforts to again and again control her, change her, he had made it so easy to hate him, so easy to hide the truth about Calista from him.

She had wanted to not care about anyone ever again in her life, had pulled the act so well that Stavros had believed all of it.

He had started a war between them, and Leah was the one who had kept feeding it. To better hide her attraction, to better fight whatever risk he presented to her emotions, she realized now. "Why did you always hate me so much?"

"I didn't hate you."

"In the beginning, I thought it was because Giannis brought me here. Because you resented my being the heiress to such a vast fortune. Which, it turned out was a big joke. You were the one, along with Dmitri, who turned Katrakis Textiles into a multimillion-dollar business. So what was it, Stavros?"

His expression shuttered instantly. "It was wrong of me, Leah. Isn't that enough?"

"No, it's not. I have a right to know. I…"

"You just…your actions—your neglect of Giannis, they reminded me of someone. But it was no excuse to—"

"Of whom?" Leah couldn't let go. Not when she was finally so close to understanding him.

"Of my father. All he cared about was himself, his next drink and how he would gain it. My mother, instead of kicking him out, instead of caring for her kids, walked out without looking back. Neither Calista nor I mattered. They left us with our grandparents who weren't equipped to raise us. All they had was a small farm. I managed fine. But Calista…

"She would watch for her at the gate for so many hours…and then one day, we got news of my father's car crash." He rubbed his face. "I remember thinking that it was a blessing for her." His mouth twisted into a bitter curve. "He died and all I could think was Calista wouldn't suffer anymore."

That said so much about his own state of mind. "And then Giannis came for you?"

"Yes, my grandfather wrote to him about my father's death. I fought so much to bring her with us. But he said he had failed with his own daughter and that he couldn't bear to fail again. I—" such pain impinged on his features that a lump formed in her throat "—I...promised her I would come back for her. And I did... It took me two years to convince Giannis. Two years to go back for her."

"What was she like when you went back?"

He frowned at her sudden question. "Why?"

"Never mind," she replied, faking nonchalance. But her head hurt, and her chest felt so tight.

My brother—I can't disappoint him, Calista had admitted once to her. Had she been afraid he would not come back? Had she been afraid to show her true self to him?

"Leah, why—"

Sinking her hands into his hair, she pulled him down for a kiss. His hands on her waist, his taste on her lips, made her feel she was owned by him. She wanted to take away his pain, to ease the confusion in his eyes every time he talked about Calista.

Drowning in his taste, she could forget all the truths bearing down upon her, she could swallow the truth forever.

His arms tightened around her while his mouth continued its passionate assault.

Just as all the other times, he was the one who finally stopped. The heated rush of their breaths mingled as he rubbed a gentle finger over her mouth.

"What was that for?"

"I have no more truths to tell. The show, I don't want to miss it, Stavros."

"Go," he commanded, a thoughtful look in his face.

"But we are not through, Leah." All kinds of promises lingered in his words.

And Leah fled.

She muddled through the darkness of the auditorium and found her seat. Up-tempo music blared as the runway dazzled with one magnificent creation after the other.

But it was mostly lost on her. He didn't join her in the adjacent seat, and Leah, still shaken by everything they had talked about, was glad for a reprieve.

Now, she wished she hadn't asked. She wished she hadn't seen that vulnerability in his eyes. That she hadn't seen the ache when he mentioned his parents.

She wished she didn't know how committed he was to his vows.

Wished she didn't understand what made Stavros the way he was. She wished she had never started on this path at all.

Because understanding Stavros meant wanting Stavros with a cloying, all-consuming madness.

Already, she saw admiration, respect in his eyes when he looked at her, she saw that flash of curiosity when she evaded his questions.

If he showed such commitment, such respect for the vows he had made to the selfish, immature girl she had been, what would he be like if she shared her fears, if she followed her heart and gave this relationship of theirs a chance?

Because, suddenly, she wanted to be that woman more than anything she had ever wanted in her life.

CHAPTER ELEVEN

WHEN LEAH HAD woken up that morning in her sun-kissed bedroom, she had already known it was a new kind of day.

Despite her efforts to protect herself, which she saw clearly now, it seemed Stavros actually saw her, the true her.

He knew that she hadn't ever touched drugs in her life. He knew that a career in fashion design meant the world to her. He knew that Giannis meant a lot to her.

It had been almost two in the morning when she had finished meeting with everyone she wanted to see. And all the while, Stavros had loomed large in her mind.

Both emotionally and physically tired and strung out by Helene's positive initial reaction to her designs, she had fallen asleep within moments after he had started the powerful engine.

It had been the best night of her life.

She felt like she was standing in front of him without a shield for the first time. It was a moment of both power and fear, for he could so easily bind her to him always, he could so easily make her...

Pushing her hair away from her face, Leah walked to the window. Fueled by that growing need to see him, she showered and dressed in a sleeveless yellow blouse and a long, flowy skirt. Braided her half-wet hair into a plait, pushed her feet into comfy flip-flops and made her way down.

She was at the last few steps on the winding staircase

that opened to the main foyer when the deafening silence finally registered.

His collar undone, his cuffs rolled back, Stavros still wore the same shirt as last night.

His hair was unkempt and his pallor a ghostly white under that olive skin. His nostrils flared as he saw her at the steps; something slithered across his face but he held her gaze, almost as if willing her to only see him, as if making her oblivious to the rest of the world.

And he was such a commanding figure that it almost worked.

Except she had lived half her life with moments like this, with that gut-twisting fear that something always went wrong when she found happiness.

Nausea pushed its way up her throat.

She gripped the balustrade so tight that her knuckles turned pale against the dark sheen but she forced herself to break his gaze and look beyond him.

Dmitri emerged from her grandfather's room, his features ravaged. A half-empty bottle of scotch dangled from his hand, and his eyes were bloodshot. He looked at her, blinked, and then walked away without another glance.

He looked like he was coming apart at the seams, the complete contrast to Stavros's frozen withdrawal, to the tight ropes with which he held himself.

"What happened?" Her words were loud, almost a scream in that dignifiedly morbid silence. She flew off the steps when he didn't answer.

Launched herself at Stavros like a crazy dog. Like an immovable wall, he absorbed all her rage, all her blows as she pummeled at him. "What happened, Stavros? Tell me or I will—"

Pulling her into him so hard that the breath was knocked out of her, Stavros hugged her. Hugged her so tight her chest hurt with the effort to breathe, her head was dizzy...

until all she could focus on was getting air into her collapsing lungs.

Only then did he loosen his hold on her. Tucking a finger under her chin he pushed it up to meet his gaze. "I'm sorry, *pethi mou*. Giannis is gone, Leah."

Leah flopped onto him, the words stealing into her with a sickening thud. "No…" she whispered, futile tears filling her eyes.

"Look at me, *galika mou*," he pleaded with such tenderness that she did.

Clasping her cheeks, he looked into her eyes. "He passed with a smile on his lips, Leah. He said he loved you, that he…he was so happy that you spent the past few days with him. I have never seen such peace in his eyes in all the years I have known him. You brought such joy to him."

"Why didn't you wake me? Why didn't you at least let me say goodbye?" She pushed away from him, bitterness and anger and pain all roping together. "He was my grandfather. You and Dmitri…I had just as much right to be with him."

The pads of his thumbs caught her spilled tears. "He insisted that I did not disturb you, Leah. Said you were not fond of goodbyes."

A sob rising through her, Leah ran back upstairs without another glance at Stavros.

He had known. Her perceptive grandfather had known how scared she had been, he had known what it had cost her to reject him again and again…

In just a few weeks, Giannis had become such a huge part of her life and now, he was gone…Leaving her alone again to mourn him.

And for once in her life, Leah didn't want to be alone, didn't want to be ruled by fear. For once, she wanted to reach for the man she desperately needed. She wanted to lean on his strength, she wanted to take everything he would give of himself, everything she had always been too scared to ask.

* * *

It was almost evening when Stavros entered Giannis's house again that day. He came to a halt in the vast foyer, the image of Leah standing at that last step, her expression of such fear and pain, the first thing he saw.

He had never seen her like that. Never heard that desperation in her tone. Over the last couple of weeks, he had accepted the fact that he had been wrong about Leah on so many levels. Yet he realized tonight that he had been no closer to truly understanding her.

She had desperately wanted him to say anything other than what he had, he knew. And the force of his own need, of his own desire to offer her anything but the hard truth, it had knocked him where he stood.

He wanted to wipe away those tears, he wanted to protect her from that grief, he wanted to…and all of it, it had nothing to do with duty.

The silence tonight was so different from all the other nights. He had done everything he possibly could to do all that Giannis had asked of him. All the arrangements had been put in place for the funeral to happen in a few days.

He was about to call for his housekeeper, instruct her to check up on Leah when she emerged from his office, rubbing her eyes. The yellow top that had looked so bright this morning was rumpled. Her hair was tangled all around her and dark circles hung under her eyes.

"Leah, were you waiting for me?"

Grabbing her hair away from her face, she pulled it tightly at the back. "Yes."

The innocent action thrust her breasts up and he swallowed his hunger.

Cristo, this was not the time for his control to shred. He was literally shivering with need.

It had been easy to offer comfort this morning. Yet now, he couldn't move, couldn't form a coherent thought. The shock of losing the one man who had ever tried to understand him, who had tried to care for him hit him hard in that moment. And he felt curiously weak, as if a strong gust of wind could knock him down.

He must have swayed because suddenly Leah was almost bowed back trying to support his weight. Her breasts rubbed against his side, her scent kicked him in the gut.

Her eyes were molten pools of concern and vulnerability as she held onto him. "You look like you are ready to fall apart. Have you sat down for a minute since last night?"

Putting her away from him, Stavros searched for his fragmented willpower. "I just need some sleep. What did you want?"

Would she ask to leave tonight? What would he do if she did?

The three months were almost up. After seeing her with Giannis these past two weeks, after talking to her about Calista, he had questions about himself.

He was drowning and he so desperately needed the very woman he had doubted.

"Nothing important. Come, I'll walk you to your room."

He smiled then, the weight on his chest lightening. "You, *pethi mou*?" She looked so lovely that his eyes hurt. "You will break in two if I so much as lean on you."

Her hands on her hips, she mock-glared at him. "I'm not as weak as I look, Stavros. If your *studly*, *macho ego* rails at accepting help from me, that's fine. But when was the last time you had something to eat? I can make something if you like."

"You're offering to cook for me?"

"Well, I can't make a three-course meal but I can manage a grilled cheese sandwich."

It was a tempting offer. Everything about her was tempting. And tonight, he was hanging on by the end of his rope.

"I'm not hungry," he said morosely, unbuttoning his shirt. She followed the movement with such wide eyes that his fingers slipped on the damn buttons. Rubbing a hand over his gritty eyes, he gave up on it. "Go to bed, Leah."

"I don't think I could sleep tonight." A shudder racked her. "I never do on such nights." The resignation in her words brought his head up. For someone so young, she had seen too much death, he realized with a pang.

They both had, a perverse thing to have in common.

She looked so vulnerable, right then, her oval face small. The urge to take her in his arms was so strong that he had to fist his hands. "There's nothing I can do for you tonight, Leah."

"No, I don't want anything, I...I didn't see you again all day and whenever I called, I was told you were busy."

Because he had instructed his secretary to not put her calls through. "I had too many things to take care of."

Wrapping her arms around herself, she nodded. "I just wanted to make sure you were okay, Stavros. And to apologize."

"Why?"

"I'm sorry for going off at you like that this morning. I'm sorry for always attacking you."

He forced a smile. "I can take it, Leah."

"It's just that...I forgot how much Giannis meant to you too."

Raising his hand, he stopped her. "Leah, it's not needed."

"Yeah?" she said with a depth of sadness. "Okay. Anyway, once I stopped crying and managed a shower, I went looking for you. Dmitri came back and wouldn't leave even though I promised I was okay. You sent him, didn't you?"

Today of all days, he didn't trust himself to be near her. That pain of hers, it had unlocked something inside him. And until he understood what, she was better left alone.

When he shrugged, she continued. "Dmitri said you hadn't said a word all night. And that you probably won't over the next few days or maybe even months. That your silence...it was the most nauseating thing in the world. That for months after Calista died, the only words he had heard from your mouth were the vows you made to me that day."

Anger roared out of him. "Bloody Dmitri needs to learn to keep his mouth shut."

"You'd rather I continue to think you as unfeeling as you make out to be, Stavros?"

"This is not your burden to bear, Leah. I have no expectations of you—"

Hurt etched into her mouth. "You will turn my life upside down because I need to be protected, but I can't even wonder what's going on with you?"

"I do not need to be protected, Leah."

"You have never wished you could unburden yourself with someone, that you could share your joy or pain or…"

"No. For as long as I can remember, I never had the indulgence to do so. If I hadn't shoved all that pain and grief away and handled things, life would have stopped for me and Calista. The way forward was the only thing left." All his life he had been alone in moments like this…and there had been far too many of them.

Had he reached his edge now?

"Well, I don't accept that. Today, of all days, when we have both lost the man who did everything he could to bind me to you, I won't accept it. This relationship he forced on you—"

"For the millionth time, he didn't force it on me." In the roiling confusion he felt, perversely, that he couldn't bear to hurt her. Not anymore. He couldn't bear for her to think he resented her in his life anymore.

Right now, she felt like the only thing that was anchoring him to his sanity. Right now, all he wanted was to take what she was offering. Right now, he wanted to lose himself. In her.

"It was not just for my benefit. He told me that, Stavros. He said you needed me just as much as he thought I needed you."

Stavros closed his eyes and dealt the blow that he knew would hurt. "But we found out that he was wrong, didn't we, Leah? It turns out you didn't need me to lock you up in a cage, you didn't need me to steal away any joy from you for five years, turns out that I was wrong about you every way… And by that same token—" he had to say it, he had to believe it, because the alternative was just unthinkable for a man who possessed no capability for emotion, knew nothing but duty "—I don't need you in my life either. It was just an old man's dream, Leah."

"Don't you dare say that!" she screamed at him, her body vibrating with rage. "Don't you dare…not tonight, Stavros."

"Leah, walk away, *pethi mou*," he warned her, past the hard lump in his throat.

It felt like he wouldn't be able to breathe for the tightness in his chest if she came any closer. It felt like the grief running through him would consume him, *and her*, if she came any closer. It felt like he wouldn't stop when he should if she came any closer.

But his stubborn, reckless wife didn't heed his warning. She never did.

"But what he said to me won't leave me alone, Stavros." Reaching him, she clasped his cheeks, stared into his eyes as if she could read into his soul.

There was nothing for her to see, nothing for her to learn. The chill that had been curling around the edges all last night and today pervaded through.

"He…loved you so much…" She ran her fingers over his mouth, her touch reverent and possessive at the same time. "When I first came to Greece, he told me so much about you that I hated you for what you had with him… and then there you were, wherever I turned, so austere, arrogant, hating me back… Any time he talked about you, his eyes lit up and this fierce pride came into his eyes, he said you only gave—" she leaned her forehead against his lips now, a long exhale racking through her "—that you... never ask anything for yourself."

Her hands vined around his midriff. "I don't want to be alone tonight. And I definitely won't leave you alone, even if you don't say a word to me."

And Stavros lost the battle against himself.

Had he even stood a chance against her from the moment he had seen her on Dmitri's yacht, he wondered.

He grabbed her wrists to push her away, to reject her embrace as every finely honed instinct warned him to. Raking her fingers over his skin, she pushed at him, until he relented. Laced their fingers together. Pulled at him until their joined hands bound her to him.

And then she took his mouth with hers, like a wave he couldn't beat down, engulfing him.

The taste of her filled him with pleasure, infused him with electricity, flew into all the open, aching places inside him.

"I'm so sorry for your loss, Stavros. You...meant so much to him. You looked after him better than his own family did."

Those words destroyed the last bit of his will, her slender body pressed to his was his undoing.

Jerking her up against his body, he covered her mouth with his. Such hunger emanated within, such need knocked at him that he devoured her soft mouth. Digging his hands into her hair, he nipped and licked, he bit and stroked, he let himself drown in her.

She gave in with a soft gasp, opened her honeyed warmth to him. The taste of her, the sound of her breathless gasps filled him up.

After five years of celibacy, he didn't have the remotest control over himself. After a lifetime of not needing anyone, the need she brought out in him, the pain she brought out in him, he had no defense against it.

* * *

His kisses were drugged, his caresses setting her on fire, his touch tearing open a chasm of longing inside her. Surrounded by his warmth, drowning in the masculine scent of him, Leah felt like she would never be alone again.

As long as Stavros continued to kiss her like this, there was no fear in her life.

There were no lies or games or duty or even the bonds of marriage between them now.

All there was was this desire in all its eviscerating and humbling honesty. In this, finally, they were equals. In this, finally, he was a man she couldn't breathe without knowing in the most intimate way and she, she was the woman who had ripped the civilized facade from him.

A sobbing protest rose through her when he tugged his mouth away from hers. The sound of his harsh breathing was little comfort. But he lifted her up until she wrapped her legs around him.

"Hold tight, *thee mou*," he commanded, his eyes so lust-glazed, his voice so rumbly that a shiver snaked up her spine.

She buried her mouth in his neck, hiding the sudden shyness that rose through her. She didn't want him to see it and stop, she couldn't bear it if he walked away because he thought she was afraid.

She was not afraid. At least not of what he would do to her. Only of the intensity of her want for him. She was afraid that whatever he did would only be the beginning of an intense yearning.

He returned to her mouth with a blistering passion that she had wanted for so long. Buried his mouth in her neck and sunk his teeth into her skin. Her legs wrapped around him, her skirt riding up to her thighs, she jerked against him, when he sucked at the soft flesh. Then he found her mouth again, nipped her lower lip this time.

Throwing her head back, she moaned loudly, pain and pleasure infusing in her very blood. And then he licked that very spot.

He carried her as if she weighed nothing, his long fingers cupping her bottom.

Heart thundering in her chest, Leah opened her eyes as she heard the thud of a door closing.

He had brought them to his office. The moment her bottom touched the oak desk, his hands reached for the hem of her blouse.

Her breathing coming so hard that it should have been a loud rattle in the room, Leah looked down. His hands disappeared under the yellow silk of her blouse. Those hair roughened wrists against her midriff, the bulge in his trousers…it was the most decadent sight she had ever seen.

"*Theos*, you're gorgeous," he groaned just as his fingers tugged her bra down with frenzied movements. And then his abrasive palm covered her breast.

"Oh…" Leah slid a little on the desk as he rubbed her aching nipples. Every time he pulled it between his fingers, her sex pulsed.

Pushing into his hand, she forgot what she had been about to say. Just his touch was sending her over the edge. Both his hands covered her breasts now. Pulling and kneading, while he murmured words she didn't understand in Greek.

"Please, Stavros…" she said, mindless in her search for release already.

All of a sudden, his curse ripped through the air and he pulled away from her.

Frustrated desire wreaking havoc on her, Leah struggled for her breath. Her breasts left alone, felt heavy, her nipples knotting with need.

"Why would you stop," she said, pushing back tears. He was so hard and warm and she was already afraid she would never want to leave. But how did she walk away from this hot magic he weaved? From how wanted and needed he had made her feel?

"Is this punishment too, Stavros?"

"Leah, look at me, *pethi mou*."

She raised a dazed gaze to him, ready to beg him to not stop. But he didn't stop. His mouth took hers in a ravishing kiss... Their tongues dueled and sucked with a frantic desperation, teeth scraped against each other until they were both panting.

"I have no protection, Leah," he murmured against her mouth finally. "I dare not risk—"

"I'm on the pill," she said in a small voice. "You dragged me to the gynecologist and stood outside her door, remember?" A flush overtook his cheeks and she milked the moment for all its worth. "It was the most humiliating moment of my life but—"

His hand covered her mouth. "No more words, *ne*?"

She pressed a kiss to the center of his palm and nodded. Continued tracing the hard mound of it to the thick veins in his wrists while her other hand explored his body.

Pushing her hands higher, he pulled her top off. Leah could hardly take in the sensations piling over her when he muttered a hoarse "Take off your bra."

In another blink, he tugged her skirt down her legs.

She sat in front of him, her breasts heavy and aching, her nipples turning into painful knots and a thong that showed more than it covered.

"*Theos*, you're going to be the death of me, Leah."

For long seconds that felt like an eternity, he only looked at her. Pulled her calf up until her foot was resting over the table, exposing the heart of her in such an indecent way that she resisted.

The hunger in his face was possessive, all-consuming, his grip over her calf unrelenting. "No, don't hide. Leah, never hide yourself from me."

Palm down, he touched her everywhere, from her shoulders bones to the valley between her breasts, from her abdomen to finally the one spot that ached for his attention.

When he covered her mound with his hand and pressed with the pad of his finger, Leah jerked, a spasm of spiraling pleasure gripping her belly.

His dark hand covering her wet warmth…fire flew in her veins. "I can smell your arousal, Leah," he whispered at her ear and she hid her face in his chest even as she reveled in his raspy voice. "That I make you feel like this…it drives me crazy in my own skin."

With a hand in her hair, he tugged her back, his grip just a little short of bruising. Dragged his mouth over her neck, leaving a trail of heat. "Every gasp you make, every moan that escapes you…tonight, they are mine. You, *pethi mou*, are all mine."

Staring into his eyes, Leah dragged him down for another kiss. "As you're mine," she whispered against his mouth.

She had never seen that blistering need in his eyes, never seen those commanding eyes darken like that.

Two fingers moved arrogantly over her nipple, plucking and rubbing while his gaze stayed on her face.

The heat with which he watched her made her feel even more exposed than her nakedness. That she would know what it felt to be possessed by him, that he would know her like no other man ever had, it filled her blood with thrill.

"Touch me," he commanded.

Still being plundered mercilessly by his mouth, Leah obeyed. If this was how alive she felt in his arms, she would be his willing slave, she thought, tucking her hand under his shirt.

He was so hot, the washboard stomach instantly clenching under her fingers, the shuddering exhale of his breath drenching her…he was as far gone in this madness as she was.

When she moved her hand down, and traced his arousal

with shaking fingers outside his trousers, he thrust his hips into her hand.

Such carnal need touched his arrogant features that Leah felt like a victor.

Leaving her breasts, he traced her rib cage, drew sensuous circles around her navel, impatiently pulled her thong off.

When he fingered her folds after what seemed like an eternity of waiting, Leah shivered violently. When he said, "Widen your legs," with such possessive intent, a feverish tremble claimed her.

When he pushed a finger, then two into her wet heat followed by a string of curses, she whimpered and dug her teeth into his shoulder.

The slick glide of his fingers was intrusive, yet addictive, his touch was alien and it felt as if she had been waiting for it, her entire life.

All of her being pulsed at her sex, on the erotic movements of his fingers as they disappeared into her aching folds, on the way he pulled her into the heat of his body…

"You are so responsive, Leah, I could do this all day long," he uttered, his other hand moving up to cover her breast again.

"I couldn't, Stavros, please…" she begged, the ever-spiraling tension too much to bear.

His fingers slicked in and out of her on a relentless tempo, stroking the fire along her nerve endings into an inferno.

She was gasping, sinking and sobbing, and she wanted more.

His hot mouth, trailing wet heat over her skin, reached her breast. With a groan that aroused her as much as his touch, he licked the aching nipple. Stroked it and played with it and did everything except what she wanted.

"Stop torturing me," she said in a voice that sounded alien to her own ears.

She felt his smile against her mouth. "Say 'please, Stavros,'" he whispered against her skin. He sounded drunk, guttural.

Joining in his game, she let go of the last layer of inhibition. She refused to beg however. Refused to bend to his will when she could demand what was hers... "Put your mouth where I want and I will put my mouth where you want it," she dared.

His curse reverberated in the dead silence, seconds before his mouth closed on her nipple.

Sensation upon sensation beat over her. Her fingers sinking into his hair, she held him at her breast. Every time he closed his mouth over her nipple and sucked, a thousand little tremors began in her lower belly.

He raked the highly sensitized point with his teeth slowly, as if he was savoring every second of it and Leah came with a scream that shattered the hot silence.

Everything inside her splintered into a thousand shards as the tremors piled on and on in mind-numbing pleasure.

Even as her voice turned hoarse with her continued gasps and screams, even as her breath left her lungs entirely, he didn't let go. His fingers continued their assault, wringing every last pull of her muscles, turning her into a mass of shuddering sensation.

When he let go of her, she flopped onto him, damp and hot and shivering, her limbs incapable of independent motion.

She heard the rasp of his zipper, followed by the quiet swish of his trousers falling and somehow, managed to look up.

The streak of color in his tight cheeks, that muscular chest falling and rising, the washboard abs, and his erection, thick and corded, lying against his belly... He was a vision, a sight she thought she would never see.

A new friction began to build between her thighs. "Wow," she said, reaching out to touch him.

The velvety weight of him was nothing like she had imagined.

Tawny irises dilated to dark pools as she wrapped her hand around it.

Tiny tremors pulsed through her sex as she rubbed the soft tip, and she marveled at her own body's reaction to him. He hissed out a breath as she tested the weight and feel of it. Cursed as she fisted him and moved up and down in a movement as instinctual as breathing.

"I'm ready to keep my word now," she said boldly, intent on tasting him, intent on driving him as mad as he had done her.

A dark smile warmed his gaze. "Yes?"

She nodded.

"I have not tasted you either, *ne*?" he said with such carnal intent that she instinctively clutched her thighs together.

But he jammed a rock-hard thigh in between. Her sensitive core rubbed against that hard thigh and a whimper escaped her.

Tugging her head back, he ravished her mouth until her lips stung. Every inch of her vibrated. "This madness, it is only beginning, *pethi mou*. Another night, we will taste each other."

He was so velvety hard in her hand and the need to know how he would feel inside her, the need to know Stavros in this raw moment...

"Do not look away, *Leah*. I want to see every expression on your face, I want to hear every sound you make."

One hand moved over her body in long, lingering strokes, over her breasts, over her stomach, and then, in one thrust that breached her virginity, in one movement that changed her forever, he entered her.

CHAPTER TWELVE

THE PAIN THAT streaked through Leah's eyes, the jagged whimper that fell from her swollen mouth arrested Stavros when he would have thrust deeper inside her. The walls of her sex were so tight around his rigid shaft, the friction so unbearably good that he had to bite the inside of his cheek to stop.

The taste of his own blood finally punctured that haze.

Slowly, as if he was waking through a fog that owned his senses, he tried to shake off the fever that clung to his skin and muscles. The dawn of truth on his lust-riddled brain was slow, excruciating.

Cristos, she was as untried in body, as innocent as she had been of all the wrongs he had attributed to her.

Another horribly wrong misstep on his part.

He had taken her so roughly, on his bloody desk of all places! For five years, he had lived like a monk and now, pushed inside her like an animal…

Shame and fury roped together inside. He wanted to pound his fist into the desk. The only thing that stopped him was the thought of scaring her.

Sweat beaded on his brow. Marshaling his thoughts by the skin of his teeth, he looked down at her. Her pinched lips, the white pallor of her cheeks…it was like a lash against his skin.

"Looks like more lies, *little wife*," he snarled.

Color returned to her cheeks and with it, that reckless

defiance that had given him sleepless nights. Like a bloody switch, he hardened even more inside her. "You assumed everything about me," she replied, her fingers digging into his shoulders.

Every inch of him felt the heat of her fingers, of her breath feathering over his skin.

He was so aroused, his body so out of his control that he closed his eyes and willed his breath to calm down. Holding her hips, he slowly pulled out, the slick slide of her walls too much temptation to resist.

She stole her hand under his shirt, searching, caressing, possessive. Like she owned him. Like he hadn't just breached her virginity like a marauding animal. Like she knew her way around a man's body.

No, his body, he corrected himself, as the feathered strokes of her fingers wreaked hell on his better intentions.

She had and she would only ever know his body, came the utterly useless and distracting thought.

Her soft fingers reached his buttocks and she dug her nails in. Sharp and hard. She pushed closer with her bottom until her breasts rasped against his chest. Pleasure burst forth in his belly and the back of his thighs and he pushed into her wet heat, despite himself.

He pulled at her hair roughly, trying to grab her attention. "Stop it," he whispered, fighting the heat building inside, the need clamoring at him to just let go. "I don't want to hurt you. *Theos*, Leah, I just…" He felt something in him clench tight against her, as if she could wreak infinite hurt on him. "I could not bear it if I hurt you anymore."

"Stavros…won't you look at me, please."

The pleading, persuasive tone would have pulled him into hell.

He opened his eyes and was lost instantly.

Her eyes glittered with raw emotion, and once again, he found himself stunned at how much she could feel, how much Leah risked despite all her lies.

In a sensuous movement that was born more of need than finesse, she brought her mouth to his. Slowly, softly, seduced him with long kisses and lingering strokes. Set her tongue to his mouth and made love to him like he had never experienced before.

Her breath was a harsh whisper against his mouth. "You will hurt me if you stop now. I started this knowing what I wanted, I started this because you finally saw me as your equal. Not a thing to be protected and controlled. Right?" When he remained silent, she buried her face in his neck, a catch in her throat. "From the moment you stood there at the airport to pick me up, all haughty, forbidding, so contemptuous—"

He groaned. "You tried to run away to Paris while Giannis waited on tenterhooks for you in Athens."

"—I had such a crush on you. I have had dreams that you would look at me like you did tonight. Please, Stavros. Tell me that I didn't imagine that look in your eyes. Tell me that you're doing this because you want me and not because you feel sorry for me or because it's your duty."

Tenderness joined fiery desire now. Tilting her chin up, he caught the tear that ran down one soft cheek. The sight of that lone tear undid him as nothing ever had. A fist could be squeezing his chest for the tightness there. "My want…for you, my need knows no reason, Leah… That I do this when I should be…" He searched for the words to say it right, searched his own feelings, as raw and strange as they were. "You make me selfish, Leah. You make me angry, and sad, and laugh and…just so unbalanced. You sink under my skin, *pethi mou*, and I can't breathe for wanting you."

Such a smile dawned on her lips that the beauty and joy in it made his breath catch.

Her shoulders tense, she slowly thrust her hips forward. "It doesn't hurt…" When he glared, she added, "…that much." Wrapping her hand around his nape possessively, she leaned in. "Give me this tonight, Stavros. Please. Give us both what we want."

That raw, unabashed request coming from that perfect little mouth was enough to shred his will.

He thrust his tongue into her mouth, falling deeper and deeper into her spell. "Tell me if it becomes too much," he commanded. "I will stop, Leah." *Even if it killed him.*

She nodded, like a good little dutiful wife when the cunning minx was anything but.

Palming her breasts, he rubbed her nipples, and the tight points curling his muscles into a new frenzy.

"You like it when I do that." She moaned into his mouth, a smile curving her lush mouth. "I could do it all day, *pethi mou*, caress your breasts, suck your nipples until you… come just from that."

With every word he said, he started moving again. And her heat welcomed him, sending a current of need through his nerve endings. "Tell me what you feel," he said, continuing to kiss her, tease her nipples with his fingers.

"No more pain," she said against his shoulder.

He thrust in again, slowly but forcefully. Reminded himself to speak again through the delirious heat enveloping him. "Now?"

"It feels achy…full…incredibly hot…" she half sobbed.

"Hold on tight to me, *thee mou*," he whispered, and pulled all the way out.

She whimpered, like a kitten denied her treat. "I feel empty now," she said, meeting his gaze, unbuttoning his shirt.

He thrust back in again, heat curling through his muscles as she slapped those long fingers over his chest. Scraped a flat nipple with her nail. "Now?"

"Oh God, Stavros…" a guttural groan escaped her.

Grabbing her hips, he locked her against him as he built up a rhythm. His climax was rushing at him, hard, explosive. Spots were beginning to dance behind his eyes.

His pulse raced, his lungs burst. Every thrust brought him closer to the edge and he couldn't contain the momentum, couldn't control his pace.

Desperation took the place of finesse, animal lust destroyed concern for her.

"Leah…I can't slow down now, *pethi mou*."

"Don't." She opened her mouth against his chest, and he jerked. Pleasure hung around on a serrated edge as she dug her teeth in, harder. "I want all of you, Stavros. I want everything you give."

Clutching her bottom, he tilted her and thrust again.

"I want to die, now. It's so much," she moaned.

"Look down," he commanded, raking through the sheer lust to find an iota of control, determined to push her to the edge one more time.

She did. A raw groan fell from her mouth.

"Touch yourself, *galika mou*." The desk shook with his thrusts, blood whooshed in his ears.

Shock flashed in her eyes. "No. I…can't. That's… just…" Her innocence tugged at him even as she undid every one of his rules with her innate sensuality.

Christos, this need for her would not stop here, would never stop consuming him.

He licked the rim of her ear, and pleaded, as he had never done before. "Imagine that it is me touching your wet heat, imagine it is me licking you there… Do it for me, Leah. *Please*."

Color streaking her cheeks, she met his gaze. "You would like it?"

"It would be the most erotic sight I would ever see."

Her mouth trembling, she snuck her hand between their bodies. Her long finger reached between them slowly. "Go on…"

Her head went back, her back arched as she stroked herself.

Stavros groaned, pumped into her, hard and fast, pleasure drenching him in sweat, robbing his breath from him.

"Come for me, Leah."

For once, in his life, the firecracker that his wife was, complied.

Pleasure burst in his veins, in his blood, in his muscles as Leah came with a long, drawn-out groan and her contracting muscles pulled at him.

His climax knocked his breath out, and his mind blanked out as he broke apart into a thousand pieces and got back together again.

Theos, he had waited because it had been the right thing to do, because his honor wouldn't let him cheat on his wife even if he didn't live with her. But, he had never expected it to be this life-changing, mind-numbing experience with her.

Leah was in his blood now, a craving in his gut. He would never have enough of her. Of her lithe body, of her glorious smile, of her sometimes infuriating words.

He had never known this exhilaration as he did with Leah, he had never felt so alive. He had never felt so needy as he did with her. He had never wanted to change, never wanted to risk his emotions as he did with her.

He had never wondered what else he had been missing out on as he did with her.

Running his hands over her shaking form, he hugged her to him. She was so fragile. And yet he felt like he was the one who was risking everything. "Leah, say something," he whispered into her scalp.

"Hmmm?" she said, lazily snuggling into him.

"You are all right?"

Her mouth opened against his chest. "I want more of you, more of this."

Laughter burst out of him. The tightness in his chest relented as she vined her arms around his waist, opened her hot mouth against his shivering muscles and kissed him. He let out a long breath, unmanned by her tenderness.

"We're only getting started, *pethi mou*," he said, enfolding her in his arms.

Over the next few weeks, Leah was so busy that she didn't have a moment to sift through the storm building through her. The night that Stavros had made such explosive love to her, she had asked if they could return home to his estate while they had been in the shower.

It was an intimacy Leah had cherished as much as the sex itself. Every little moment with Stavros, she realized, taught her more about herself.

He had stopped midway, his hands incredibly gentle as they washed her. After he had carried her to the en suite bathroom of his bedroom, turned on the shower and demanded to know if she was hurting anywhere. Had looked so vulnerable when he had said he didn't usually behave like a rutting animal.

How he believed that she could think that of him when he had honored the vows he had made to her, she didn't know. But his concern had touched her on a fundamental level.

The first thing the next morning, they had returned here. Once the servants had unpacked for her, and he had carried her from her bedroom to his, declaring in that arrogant tone that she wouldn't sleep anywhere else but his bed, only then had she realized that she had called it home.

But that's what his estate felt like to her.

Home.

She had been accepted to present at the Independent Fashion Week in New York in September. When she had told him after Helene had called her personally, he had smiled at her, fierce pride glinting in his eyes, and told her that he wasn't the least bit surprised.

After a few meetings with Helene and another fashion

director, the scale and the scope of her collection was even more than she had dreamed. She had added four more designs to it.

She was on such a constant high, on a ride that only kept going higher and higher that she didn't want to stop even for a moment to see where it was that she was going or how long she would be able to sustain that momentum.

She worked twelve, fourteen hours to finish her first collection, which was turning out to be better than she had ever imagined. Models came in almost every day now for trials, she had two assistants helping her with the final touches, gowns that were being resized and resewn, and then pressed once finalized…

At the end of the day, she fell into bed exhausted. She put off questions about the future. She ran around the estate, she worked with such feverish compulsion that Stavros had one day locked her in his bedroom after she had almost collapsed in her workroom.

But even through the frenzy of the creative drive that gripped her through the day, the best parts were at night.

Intense, hot, turning-her-inside-out nights with Stavros.

It was as if they were both determined to assuage a hunger of a lifetime every single night. It didn't matter what time he flew back from Athens, it didn't matter that sometimes her own work kept her past midnight, he brought her to his bed at all manner of times.

Sometimes, they would both be too exhausted to do nothing but sleep wrapped up in each other, and he would wake her after the edge of sleep was gone. Sometimes, he woke her up in the early morning and was moving inside her before she was completely awake.

He was insatiable, possessive, his touch incredibly addictive.

The one time he had stayed overnight in Athens, a strange panic had gripped her. Suddenly, it was as though she had lost her anchor. She had woken up to the sounds of rotor blades the next morning, her breath painfully hovering in her throat. Had waited for him to come to her.

Morning had given way to noon, and then to a gorgeous sunset. He was busy, he had sent a message when she had inquired.

Even loathing that she was losing some unknown battle of wills, she had gone looking for him once the estate had settled down for the night. She had found him in his office, in the middle of a conference call, his gaze settling on her with a possessive hunger. Yet, he hadn't moved.

She had had the strangest feeling that he had kept away on purpose. As if it was a test he was conducting. As if he wanted to prove something to himself.

An experiment she had no interest in, she had realized, a test she had lost even before it had begun. How dare he deny her after he had made her addicted to him?

So she had teased him when he had made no move to interrupt the call.

Brazen and bold, she had slowly stripped every single piece of clothing from her body even as he was still on the video call. He had looked at her with darkening eyes, daring her to continue.

Of course, she had never been able to resist a dare, especially when it came to riling, or in this case, arousing Stavros.

He had even held out for a few minutes.

Her skin on fire, her body craving him, she had refused to back down. She had touched herself, her breasts first, rolling her aching nipples between her fingers, imagined it was those rough fingers of his. Like he had begged her to do that first night.

Dark color streaked his cheeks, and the pen he had been holding to make notes had clattered to the ground. But still, he hadn't given in.

Her throat had felt like parched paper, her grasp on her emotions tenuous at best. She had become a slave to his will. Even worse, she had become a slave to her own need for him.

Throwing her hair back, as she had seen one of the models wearing her own creation do, she had strutted farther into the room. He had lasted another two seconds before he had minimized the screen, marched to her, picked her up, called her his doom, and taken her against the wall, even as the call was going on.

All the while his mouth had covered hers, swallowing her moans and finally the sound of her climax. There had been no finesse to his raw thrusts, there had been nothing of his will left by the time he had climaxed, his skin damp to her touch.

She had won that day. But the fear that she wouldn't another day, another moment, gathered like a black cloud. Because as invested as he was in their madness, she knew he was retreating. As if she and his desire for her, they were a rope that was slowly binding him and he...he was struggling against it.

He refused to discuss the state of their little deal. Every time she tried to talk of the past or the future, he evaded her or worse, seduced her. And the coward that she was, Leah let him be. Settled for the warmth of his arms, for the heat of his caresses, for the fiery intensity of his passion.

"Are you happy?" she had asked him one morning when he had brought her breakfast in bed.

He had covered her body with his, taken her mouth in such a tender kiss that it had brought tears to her eyes. "I don't know about happy," he had said against her mouth with that trademark honesty. The question seemed to have thrown him, but lost in the magic his mouth weaved, Leah hadn't cared. "But I've never felt more alive, *agape mou*."

There was something disconcerting about that answer, she remembered thinking.

Almost a month passed by like that. And from the dreamy, drugged state, something else emerged. A tiny sliver of fear for the future. Of what she was letting happen, of what it was going to hold for her and Stavros.

For a few weeks, she had been hinting about going to Paris for a small fashion event that Helene had mentioned. It was like puncturing the bubble they seemed to exist in, but she pushed the matter anyway. Sooner or later, they would have to emerge from it and for her part, she wanted him to acknowledge their relationship outside of his estate.

Finally, the night before the event, he had given in. Surprised her by joining her the next evening. And any thoughts she had that their relationship would change evaporated in the week they had been in Paris.

Leah dragged him on a tour of the beautiful city and shopping while he dragged her back to their luxurious hotel suite on the Champs-Elysées every time the mood struck him. Which was much too often, she had complained once laughingly.

But she hadn't denied him, not once. She was just as addicted to him as he seemed to be with her.

They had been in Paris a week when, one evening, someone knocked quite rudely on the outer door of their suite.

Leah laughed, and hid her face in Stavros's chest while he continued to lick and kiss her breasts with no thought to the caller. Soon, she was as lost as he was when he lazily pushed into her and struck a slow, mind-numbing pace toward release. The elegant side table, whose design she had only remarked on earlier, bumped against the wall as his thrusts became harder and faster.

"What you do to me, Leah," he whispered, leaning into her.

She kissed his sweat-beaded brow when he suddenly stilled.

And Leah heard it—the sound of footsteps coming closer toward their bedroom.

In a movement that was both blurry and genius— because she couldn't even move a finger, Stavros was off her and pulling on his sweatpants. Had just covered her naked form with a sheet when the double doors burst open.

Arrogantly leaning against the wall, Dmitri surveyed them, the wickedest grin curving his sinful mouth. Heat bloomed over every inch of her as that dark, slumberous gaze took in the state of their undress and their still uneven breaths.

Stavros's curse, filthy and loud, should have colored the room blue before he dragged her behind him. "Forgotten your manners again, Dmitri?"

Such blistering scorn filled his voice, yet Leah, peeking from behind his shoulder, only saw it bounce off Dmitri's amused smile. Being the complete opposites they were, Leah had never understood their friendship. Only that it was inviolate.

"Of all your dresses, I think this suits you best, *pethi mou*," Dmitri offered with an outrageous wink and Leah couldn't help but smile.

A growl emanated from Stavros and her gaze flew to him. It was a savage sound she would never associate with him of all the men in the world. His passion was insatiable, never-ending but he hid it under such a civilized facade that she couldn't believe it the first few days.

He did, and made her do, the wickedest things in bed—which she did with the same spiraling hunger as he did, but outside of bed, outside of sex, he was still far too private.

She knew that, in the past month, Dmitri had wanted to see them, more than once. Wanted to join them either for a dinner, or even for a lazy afternoon at Stavros's estate. But he had said no every time in that arrogant tone of his. Hadn't even bothered to make an excuse.

It was almost as though he didn't want Dmitri to see them as a couple.

Was he still ashamed of her, she wondered now, trying to stave off the hurt it caused. *Or did he think it a tempo-*

rary madness that he didn't want to share with his closest friend?

"I wouldn't have had to disturb your connubial bliss," Dmitri drawled completely unaffected by Stavros's rising temper, "if you had not done the disappearing act on me. I had to half seduce your location out of your poor secretary. Very uncharacteristic of you, Stavros. Your staff is petrified that you might be dying."

Stavros turned to her. "Do you want to get dressed, Leah?"

"She should hear this. I wouldn't have barged in just for anything, Stavros."

"What is it, Dmitri?"

"Alex Ralston showed up on my yacht today. My security tried to grab him but they weren't successful."

Suddenly cold, Leah shivered. Throwing his arm around her, Stavros pulled her into his warm body.

Alex had been Calista's on-and-off boyfriend. "Alex… you sent him to jail after Calista…"

"We found that he was the one selling drugs that day. He had a long record of possession and substance abuse," Dmitri replied while Stavros remained stubbornly silent.

"I thought you did that because…" The words trailed off Leah's lips as she realized how absurd she sounded.

Alex had been the one who had given them to Calista? Charming, easygoing Alex? And in contrast, Stavros had seemed such a monster in her head.

"Get dressed, Leah. Let me talk to Dmitri alone."

She was so much in panic that she didn't even say a word. Something flickering in his eyes, Dmitri hugged her, sheet and nakedness and all.

After all these years, what did Alex want now?

CHAPTER THIRTEEN

Stavros had been expecting something to strike at the haze in which he had been living for the past month. Something that would wake him up from the dreamlike state he had been functioning in with Leah. Something so painfully real, so achingly raw, it was bound to end.

He expected the novelty of making love to her to wear off. He expected the high of being around her, the high that came with her laughter, with her irreverent humor, with how easily she gave of herself and how possessively she demanded of him, to end at some point.

He expected the amazing light and joy that had pervaded him, even as he had tried to tether and control it, to fizzle out.

Because life didn't work like that, did it? At least, not his.

It didn't carry so much joy, so much laughter, so many emotions that had overthrown him the last month. It never had such gnawing hunger, such desperate need to grasp what he could, such panic-ridden drive to control it so that he didn't become its slave.

But he didn't think it would come in such a way. He hadn't thought it would rip his heart out like this and leave him gasping.

That it would wreak on him an avalanche of hurt and inadequacy and pain.

He had thought Dmitri uncharacteristically foolish to even indulge Alex Ralston's demand to talk to Stavros.

Yet, he had just disconnected the call with Alex, a video call that the thug had insisted on.

Nausea whirled in his gut at the things Alex had said about Calista. It was like hearing stories about a stranger, not his sister at all.

All he had known of Calista had been a front, a lie. A lie that had been neatly supported by Leah for so many years. Because Leah had known it all.

And in the sinking morass of his grief, that betrayal cut the deepest. Leah had known and hadn't whispered a word to him. Even when he had asked it of her.

"Stavros?" Dmitri nudged him.

"Locate him, Dmitri." He stood up with such force that the desk rattled. "He can't go to the media with this. *Theos*, this is Calista… I don't want her name besmirched like this."

"I will stop him. Stavros…it's not your fault. Calista… whatever Ralston told you about her, you couldn't have known. You did everything you could to help her."

"I should have known. All along, she had so many problems and I…" A growl escaped his throat.

"Have you ever thought that some of us are beyond help, Stavros? Too broken to be fixed? Giannis said she was just a child when your mother walked out. Whatever Calista needed, you didn't have it."

"She needed to be loved, Dmitri. And I couldn't do it. I didn't know how. Not then, not now."

He was the one in pain, and yet Dmitri looked pale. He kept shaking his head as if he could see into Stavros's head. "Her behavior is not your fault."

"I wish I could forgive myself as easily as you, Dmitri," he said, hating himself, hating Dmitri for being so understanding.

He couldn't numb the gnawing in his gut as the truth solidified. He had never had what it took to begin with.

Was that why he had clung so tightly to doing what was

right? Because he hadn't possessed, hadn't ever known, his heart?

Beneath Leah's betrayal, beneath the shock of learning his sister's truth, only one thing remained.

You are made of stone.

How right Leah had been... If he had ever known it once, he didn't remember. He didn't know if he had buried it deep so that his parents' indifference, their negligence didn't hurt.

He had never understood Calista, never saw past the facade his sister presented because he had never understood her fears, her pain, her joy. Every time she had mentioned their parents, every time she had expressed her confusion, he had only pushed her to move on, had brushed her away believing that they were better off without them.

Because he hadn't wanted to dwell on it, because it would mean acknowledging all the wrongs they had done to them, it would mean letting them be a part of who they were.

Again and again, he had closed himself off to her grief, her pain. Until she had decided that he would never understand? Until she had decided, *like Leah*, that he didn't have the capability to understand? The capability to love?

In the end, his parents had robbed him of everything.

Even if he forgave Leah's lies, what did he possess to give her? How long before she would realize the truth? How long before she realized that he had never known and would never understand love?

That he would never know how to give it and take it.

It was two hours before Stavros returned to their suite, two hours in which Leah had become half-crazy wondering what was going on. One look in his eyes, and her heart skidded to her gut.

"Pack your bags. You're catching a flight to New York in a few hours."

"What? The fashion week isn't for another fortnight..."

He stood only a foot away, yet it could have been a thousand miles. Why wouldn't he look at her?

"It is better for you in New York rather than here with Ralston around. Apparently, he's very much interested in hearing how I've mistreated you."

"But all my stuff is…" She stopped, his words slowly registering with her.

His cell phone rang and he looked at her finally. "I will ensure that Rosa packs up your stuff with utmost care."

Rosa was going to pack her stuff, she was going to leave for New York…

Leah stared at the empty space he left behind for a few seconds. The shock slowly blunted, bringing in its wake utter panic.

Throat dangerously close to tears, she found him in the study that offered a breathtaking view of the Eiffel Tower.

He was on the phone, listening, but his gaze stayed on her face. And that's when Leah noticed the white pallor to his skin.

She would have welcomed his blistering contempt, or even his lacerating fury. But the resignation in his gaze… As if he had lost something precious. As if he had finally given up.

The minute he disconnected the call, she stepped inside.

"If he comes for me, he has to get through you, doesn't he?" she demanded, anger coming to her rescue. She wouldn't let him treat her like this again. Not after the last month.

He looked up, a bitterness curving his mouth. "I'll be busy trying to stop him from taking the story to the media, from turning my life and Calista's…and yours into a cash cow."

"What?" she said, fear spewing into her words now.

"If you go to New York, you'll be free to do as you please. I know how much you don't like being told what to do. I'll make sure Ralston doesn't follow you."

"Why does it sound like you're sending me away?" She sounded desperate, pitiful, but she didn't care. It seemed she had no armor left.

He stood up from the chair, his every movement precise, his skin tautly pulled over those sharp features. There was nothing anymore of the man she had known this last month. The man who had smiled, laughed, kissed her, the man who had looked at her as if he would drown if he didn't possess her one more time, nothing.

It was as if he was pulling himself back, word by word, second by second, until he became that Stavros she hated again.

Her gut twisting, she walked around the huge desk until he was forced to look at her. Placing her hands on his chest, she asked, "What did I do this time?"

He grabbed her wrists to push her away. But she didn't let go. She would never hold him again if she let go, the fear clamored through her. "Tell me what's going on, Stavros. Or I swear I'll…" she broke off on a sob.

"You'll what, Leah? Tell a new lie? You have won." He became stiff, like he was a statue who possessed no feeling, no weakness. "I'll sign the divorce papers, release your inheritance as soon as possible. You are just Leah Huntington again." His gaze moved over her features with a hunger she knew he would deny. For all his withdrawal, she had the strangest feeling that he wasn't untouched. That he was struggling just as she was.

Or it was the delusion she really wanted to cling to, she thought pitying herself.

"There's nothing binding you to me or to Katrakis Textiles now."

Her breath whooshed out of her in a painfully long exhale. Legs shaking beneath her, Leah grabbed the table. Tears pooled in her eyes and spilled over. Just breathing became a chore. "You're punishing me again…"

"Punishment, *pethi mou*? No. I'm finally freeing us

both. Giannis is gone, and you've proved beyond doubt that you can take care of yourself, *ne*? What is left of our relationship, if it could be called that, if we take away my duty and your lies, Leah?"

"The last month—"

"Last month has been nothing but sex. Five years of celibacy and you…it would mess with any man's head, even a stone like me."

That he would reduce the last month like that, that he would cheapen what they had shared so easily…she couldn't even breathe.

Fear stole coherence from her. Slowly, she thought back to how the dreadful afternoon had begun. "What did Alex say?"

"Threatening to go the media with a colorful story about Calista and her monster of a brother who neglected her and then married the heiress… The pictures he has of her, the horrible things he's threatening to say about her…" Restrained violence simmered in him as he moved away from her. As if he didn't trust himself to be near her. "The parties, the drinking, the men… *Cristos*, I didn't know my sister at all, did I? And you knew it all along." He turned toward her again, accusation and pain in his eyes.

"She begged me not to tell you, Stavros. Every time you found us at some party, she would beg me to leave her out of it. She asked me to cover…just once more. When she saw you, when she was with you, she…she wanted to be perfect. She was desperate to not lose you. Desperate to not lose your love. She was afraid that you would…"

"All your arguments with me, if you had thrown it once in my face that she was the one—"

The calmer he got, the more she panicked. "I didn't realize how bad it had gotten until that night. Stavros, I was immature, foolish. I told you, I didn't know that she was using. I feel sick to my stomach when I think I could have helped, when I could have—"

"What about the last few weeks, Leah? What about when I begged you for the truth about her? What reason could you possibly have to lie after all these years? Were you afraid that I would punish you for her actions? Even after these few weeks, were you just looking out for yourself?"

Her heart hammered away in her chest, her knees trembled beneath her and all she wanted was to be held by him, to see him smile, to do whatever she could to remove that betrayal, that pain from his eyes.

And just like that, the truth struck Leah. In that darkpaneled study in a majestic hotel in one of the loveliest cities in the world, with Stavros looking at her with utter resignation, it came to her.

She was in love with Stavros. A few months ago, she would have cackled hysterically at the prospect. And yet, had she ever truly stood a chance against the man she had discovered him to be?

Despite all the wrongs done to him as a child, he had done his duty. He could cajole and love and support as fiercely as he followed his duty, he could care, even though it was through actions and not words...

Calista had been so wrong in not trusting him, in doubting his love, so painfully unknowing of her own brother... But Leah understood him finally, she knew what a complex and honorable man her husband was.

And knowing Stavros meant loving Stavros, loving his generous heart, his sense of duty, even his rigidly autocratic dictates.

Why else had she risked everything she had always been scared of, this past month, how else would she have thrown herself into this madness with such relish... "After all these years, I didn't think the reasons for Calista's death mattered anymore. Not when I was finally..."

"When you were finally getting what you wanted," he finished and utter fury filled her.

She gasped as it unfurled inside her, this new feeling, sinuously breathing courage into her very veins, filling her with a tremendous energy.

Reaching him, she refused to let him dismiss her so easily. "When, *finally*, you saw me for what I was, and let me see what kind of a man you were. I thought I should leave the past where it was. I thought...I could have—"

"Your wants, your needs—it's all about you, isn't it, *pethi mou*?"

"For years, it has been, yes. All I thought of since stepping in Athens was protecting myself from pain, from ever having to mourn another loved one again. But not anymore. For the first time in my life, I lied, not for myself, but for you. I lied to protect you, to spare you from this pain of knowing Calista's reality.

"I lied because I...care about you. I lied because, somehow, you gave me the courage to live without fear, I lied because you made it impossible to not love you."

His skin pulled into a taut mask, he looked as if she had dealt him an invisible blow. Everything in her scrunched into a painful ball as Leah realized that her words, somehow, had only hurt him even more.

"Say something, Stavros," she said desperately.

"I didn't realize until today how ill-suited we are for each other, *pethi mou*. Even if I continue this charade in the name of Giannis, it won't be long before we rip each other into shreds. Before there's nothing but pain left."

The bridge of his nose, the sculpted planes of his face, the stubble that was already coming in...it hurt to look at him. "Is that any worse than what you're doing now?" A shuddering gasp left her. "Somehow, I doubt that you can get any more cruel, any more heartless, Stavros."

"Then you know why our farce of a marriage needs to end," he finally said after what felt like an eternity of hell. "You have your freedom. Goodbye, Leah."

* * *

For the first time since Giannis had brought him to Athens years ago, Stavros did not return to work after Leah left.

He let Dmitri's calls go unattended, told his assistant to cancel everything indefinitely, heard from his head of security that a particularly treacherous board member, a distant cousin of Giannis who had always resented that Stavros and Dmitri were the topmost shareholders on the Katrakis board, was planning a coup to take over.

Rumors swirled about that Dmitri and he had fallen out, causing the stock for Katrakis Textiles to sink.

But Stavros, try as he did, still clinging to his wretched sense of duty, couldn't give a damn. He and Dmitri had slaved night and day to build it into a multimillion dollar industry for over a decade, given it their all because they had wanted Giannis's legacy to mean something…because they had both wanted something to anchor their lives.

And yet, he did not care if it all crashed and burned. All he wanted to do was shrug off the world and retreat. And he did.

Yet, wherever he turned, there were signs of Leah at his estate.

From the workers at the vineyard to the seamstress who asked if Leah was taking New York by storm, from the trails she had loved running through to the small, inconsequential things she had left lying around the house, like her iPod. She was everywhere.

She was under his skin, in his every breath, she had somehow become an irrevocable part of himself.

The peace he had found on his estate, the rules he had set in place all his life, everything was shattered. He felt empty within and he hadn't even known that he had something so precious.

It was as if Leah had breathed life into him, showed him what it was to laugh, love and live.

For days, he let himself remember every bleary moment

from when his mother had left to when his father had died, and he grieved for Calista. Grieved for the innocence he had never had. For days, he sat in the study in his estate, wandered into Leah's empty workroom.

And slowly, her words gained strength in him, shifted and morphed his very view of himself.

For the first time in my life, I lied, not for myself, but for you, Stavros. I lied to protect you, to spare you from this pain.

I lied because I...care about you. I lied because, somehow, you have given me the courage to live without fear, I lied because you made it impossible to not love you.

Leah loved him, she had protected him. When had anyone ever thought of him like that?

The Leah that wouldn't leave him alone the night of Giannis's death, the Leah that had so innocently and full of hope, asked him if he was happy, the Leah that had teased and aroused him with such stark, possessive need...that Leah who refused to let him deny what they both wanted, needed when he had worried that it was becoming an obsession, a madness, the Leah that had held him tightly, when in the aftermath of making love to her he had confided that he didn't remember how his mother looked, the Leah that had believed in the sanctity of marriage...

That woman was worthy of a fight, was worthy of a man he could be.

She had made him love for the first time in his life, she made him care, had made him live for himself, made him want with such gnawing hunger.

Had given him a taste of happiness, of pain, of ache, of loss.

She had made him feel everything he had shied away from his whole life. And he wanted to live like that again. He couldn't go back to being an automatic machine.

Shaking at the very chill in his bones, he leaned his forehead against the glass door looking out into the estate.

In a moment of utter desolation he had admitted to Giannis that night that he had been wrong about Leah, that he had ruined her life. Even facing death, Giannis had smiled, had said that Leah needed him, that he, Stavros, was a man worthy of her... Those words pushed through to the fore, crushing his self-doubt.

Maybe he hadn't deserved Leah five years ago.

But now, facing his own incapability to love Calista as she had needed, and accepting that, despite his every effort, his parents had somehow damaged him, forgiving himself for not loving Calista as she had needed, he deserved Leah now.

He deserved to be happy, he deserved to think about himself after a lifetime of thinking about everyone else.

Suddenly, Stavros couldn't live without telling Leah that, couldn't bear that she was thousands of miles away. Not when he loved her so much.

CHAPTER FOURTEEN

HER COLLECTION AT the Independent Fashion Week in New York had gone better than Leah could have imagined in her wildest dreams. Her designs had been called modern, colorful, yet sophisticated. Just last week, with Helene's advice, she had invested a load of money into creating a lookbook that incorporated line sheets, one that gave buyers and fashion magazine editors a view into her brand.

After a crazily hectic two weeks, she had returned to Athens. When she had knocked at Mrs. Kovlakis's door and requested the keys to her old flat and the dragon had simply handed them over, she had been both shocked and relieved. One look at the news and she found Dmitri and Stavros and herself at the front and center of it.

Hiding and barely eating, she had slept for a week. All of a sudden, she would find herself awake and looking at her phone, before she realized she was waiting for his call.

Had he so thoroughly washed his hands of her? Had she truly meant nothing to him?

She had cried until she had been disgusted with herself, moped around the flat until one afternoon, Dmitri had almost broken the door down when she hadn't heard his knocking.

He had taken her out to lunch, plied her with food until she had eaten enough for a month, inquiring if she needed anything.

Did he send you? she had asked, pitifully desperate.

No, he had said with unflinching honesty. *You've truly proved yourself to him.*

Words she would have embraced before now seemed like punishment.

At which point, she had cried and he had sighed and hugged her, and point-blank asked her if she meant to spend the rest of her hard-won freedom like a howling puppy, if she meant to spend the rest of it as the discarded wife of Stavros Sporades, hiding from the world.

Hating him and loving him for it, she had decided enough was enough. After fighting Stavros tooth and nail, she refused to let him win, refused to let herself become a shadow.

She had her whole life in front of her. She had decisions to make about where she would operate, about staff to hire, preparations to make for the winter collection, about her finances and how much of her inheritance she could invest in her business and how much she needed to save for a rainy day. She couldn't live in some distant, unfamiliar corner of the world because Stavros was here.

The freedom to make her own choices, once she had begun, was heady, exhilarating.

More than one designer house approached her with offers to join them. Loath to compromise her creative vision, she refused all of them in a bold move.

Just as she finally embraced the fact that she was a shareholder in her grandfather's textile companies, that she was part of his legacy.

She had walked into the legendary Katrakis offices in downtown Athens and attended her first board meeting, her heart threatening to rip out of her chest at the thought of facing Stavros.

That Stavros was absent and she was present created a stir that had made Dmitri smile wickedly. Whispers and innuendoes abounded large, about Dmitri, about Stavros, about her. And the worst of all, about the state of her marriage to Stavros.

It had taken everything she had possessed to get through the day. Especially after she received a message from Stavros's assistant that he would like to meet her before she left on her trip to Milan the next day. The requisite paperwork would be sent to her lawyer if she could provide a name, she had been told.

Nausea rising in her throat, Leah had headed straight to the ladies' room.

That was that then. He was going to divorce her. After five years, the bond between them would be broken. He would be free of her and she…of him. He would not be hers, even for a moment, ever again.

That night she went to bed, an ache in her gut.

She dreamed of him, intense, vivid dreams that woke her from restless sleep, breathing hard and aching, damp with need, inconsolable that he would never hold her again.

Violently furious that after demanding that she show him the real her, he had not believed the biggest truth she had ever told him.

He didn't deserve her, she decided, the lie hollow to her own ears.

Leah arrived at Stavros's office thirty minutes after ten, having finally fallen into a fitful sleep in the early hours of the morning. Her head hurt, her muscles ached from having thrashed so much.

So when she grabbed the handle and pushed the door open, she was feeling particularly bloodthirsty, as he put it once.

There was no one in his office room. Her heels clicking on the marble floor, she walked around. Her nape prickled and she turned.

Standing at the entrance to his private suite, Stavros studied her.

He looked as he always did, arrogant, implacable, larger than life, except for the haunted look in his eyes. He wore jeans that molded those powerful thighs and a gray shirt that stretched against the muscled expanse of his chest.

He was so achingly gorgeous, so painfully beautiful that her throat closed up. She just stared at him hungrily for several minutes.

"I found the land you were looking at to build a factory."

Leah flinched at the sight of him, at his raspy voice, at his blank expression. That was the first thing he said to her? Not even hello?

"I don't need your help," she said flippantly. "Where are your lawyers?"

"We don't need them."

"Then why did you summon me here? Why not just sign the papers and be done with it? Or have you gotten addicted to me begging you for things like cash, sex and the minimum courtesy that you believe me?"

Something slumberous glinted in his gaze. "I don't remember you begging me for sex."

"Maybe because it held no meaning to you except for relief after five years of…" He prowled toward her with such dangerous intent that she stopped talking.

"I remember every moment, *pethi mou*. I just don't have a memory of you begging me for it. All those nights, and days, *not once*." A dark current tinged his words as if he was very much fantasizing the prospect of it now. "You teased me, you taunted me, you seduced me…and I just gave in every time, your willing slave."

"I'm leaving," she said, his strange mood making her weak everywhere.

He blocked her way. "Dmitri told me that you attended the board meeting. That you caused quite a stir. A walking powerhouse, that's what he called you."

She sent a silent thanks to Dmitri for hiding the ugly crying from Stavros.

"Are you surprised? I will not slink away from what is mine like a coward anymore. I will sit on the Katrakis board, I will launch my label from Athens. I will not hide as if the fiasco of our marriage is my fault.

"I won't let you browbeat me into anything I don't want to do ever again."

He looked tortured, his mouth pinched. "Forcing you to marry me was the biggest mistake I have ever made, *thee mou*. I can't believe—"

She had no idea that she had thrown herself at him. That with her weight and fists she had pushed them farther into the rear room of his private suite. Pain, and ache and a bone-deep hunger, everything deluged her.

Tears flew freely down her cheeks as she continued attacking him.

How dare he call knowing her a mistake? How dare he hurt her when all she had wanted was to protect him? How dare he be so heartless when she cared so much about him?

"Do you, *agape mou*?" he whispered when she hit him in the gut and she realized she had been screaming the words at him. "Do you care so much, Leah?"

She wouldn't say it again, wouldn't beg for his love when it had to be hers, when it was what she deserved.

"Leah, *pethi mou*, look at me," he begged continuously, yet she couldn't stop.

She was so afraid that he would disappear if she stopped, so afraid that she would wake up and realize it was a dream. That she would be achingly alone again.

"I'm sorry, *yineka mou*," he whispered, without even trying to stop her. "I'm so sorry that I sent you away. I'm so sorry that I didn't listen to you."

"You're a heartless bastard and I should hate you," she said, with another push and then they were falling into the bed.

"*Theos*, no more than I hate myself, Leah," he said on a ragged whisper.

Her breath jarred out of her as Leah landed on top of him. Fear and relief gave way to something else as her mouth lodged in his neck and his arousal pressed against her belly. Moving of their own accord, her legs straddled him, until his hardness pressed against her heated core. Her thighs shivered with the repressed need to ride him.

Her hands in his hair, Leah lifted her head and looked into his eyes.

Their harsh breaths thundered in the silent room, joined by the whisper of the satin sheets.

"I want you to sign those papers and get the hell out of my life. I want to never see you again."

"I can't," he said, sounding almost regretful.

"I do hate you," she said again, every inch of her desperately craving what he could give.

Only him. Always, only Stavros.

She closed her eyes to lock away the tears and touched her mouth to his.

Familiar and intense, the taste of him made her shiver violently, sent a jolt of electricity through her very veins. She continued kissing him softly until her heart was beating a loud tattoo against her chest, until tears blocked her throat again.

Until all she could touch, breathe and feel was him, until she could be sure that he was here, with her.

"I will never divorce you, Leah. I will never set you free."

What new madness had he thought of now?

Rolling away from him, she began to slide off the bed. His hand on her ankle, Stavros pulled her back onto the sheets in a deft movement. Struggling to get free, she squealed. And gasped when he covered her body with his.

His weight pressed her into the bed, stealing her breath. Clutching her eyes closed, Leah fought the craving that burst within her belly like a fire. Her arms literally ached to hold him, her body on fire to be possessed by him.

"I have missed you so much, *agape mou*," he said, shuddering harshly.

She felt his mouth probe hers softly, slowly, as if asking for permission. Holding her wrists at her head with one hand, he pressed little kisses on the seam of her lips, his warm breath drenching her.

In a needy, hoarse voice that unlocked every last fear in her, he punctured the kisses with words in Greek.

"Please, *pethi mou*. Let me in." He swiped at her mouth with his tongue, his body pressing into hers. "I would drown if you would not let me kiss you, Leah, I would stop breathing if you gave up on me now. My life is no life without you in it. Until you brought it to me, I have not known love. Do not take it away now, Leah."

And the tender gesture, the unvarnished love in his words undid her. Twining her arms around his neck, Leah gave in. He kissed her as if he were truly drowning, with desperate desire.

Lips scraped against teeth, limbs tangled, breathing was secondary as the fire between them consumed them.

"Tell me that I haven't lost you already. Tell me that you will teach me how to love you, Leah. *Theos*, it is all I want."

When she remained silent, he whispered, "I love you, Leah."

The declaration rang around in the silence, and slowly Leah opened her eyes. The truth of it shone in his eyes, rendering him acutely vulnerable. It was a look she had never thought to see on Stavros's face.

"You sent me away without a thought to me. I couldn't believe how cruel you were, how much it hurt," she said, her mouth trembling. "How easily you could break my heart, reject my love..."

"The news about Calista devastated me, I thought I could never love you like you need to be loved... I stomped on my own feelings, Leah."

"But you do know, Stavros. You don't say it in words,

you won't share your thoughts, but your actions…they speak so much. You are incredibly giving, caring, even if you drive me up the wall with your arrogance."

He traced a finger over her mouth, such tenderness in his eyes that Leah couldn't breathe. "I will never stop loving you, nor will I ever give you up. I—"

She ran shaking fingers over his brow, pushing back his hair. "When I'm with you, I'm unafraid. All I want is to take risk upon risk, all I want is to live and love you."

"Then let's do it, *pethi mou.*"

Burying her face in his neck, Leah nodded, her head dizzy with euphoria, fear beating a tattoo. He pushed them both off the bed and brought her to the edge of it. While she shivered all over from the intent on his face, he knelt in front of her.

Looked at her with such love in his eyes that fresh tears fell on her cheeks.

"Will you marry me again, Leah?" he asked against her lips. "Will you…choose to spend the rest of your life with me, *pethi mou*?"

Leah buried her mouth in his throat, swallowed the tightness in hers. "Yes, Stavros. I'll marry you… Tomorrow, if you can arrange it."

"No, not tomorrow," he said, tugging her face up to his.

"Why not? Are you having second thoughts already?"

The ache in his eyes undid her. "I…want you to have the wedding you've always wanted. I want to take you out a few times. I want to do all the things you might have wanted to do before you married… I want you to take all the time you want…and until then…" He looked into her eyes and the love she saw there sent her heart to bursting.

She shook her head, instantly understanding how his mind worked. Scooting closer to him, she straddled him and they both groaned. "No… I can't sleep without you by my side. I can't bear it if you—"

"You will see me every day. When I make love to you again, you will have chosen to be my wife this time."

Something in his tone told her how important this was to him. That she marry him, that she become his wife because she loved him. "Three months," she moaned, tugging his lower lip with her teeth. "Let's set a date for after three months and no later. I don't have your patience or your willpower…"

He took her mouth in a hungry kiss that set fire to her claim… "Willpower, *yineka mou*? Waiting for you to walk toward me in your wedding dress…that's the only thing that will keep me going."

EPILOGUE

Three months later

STAVROS HAD NO idea that three months could feel like an eternity. *Theos*, he must have been insane to set the rule he had because touching Leah and kissing Leah without taking her had been an exercise in torture.

But in the same breath, he was also extremely glad that they had waited. Because Leah was worth every smile, every ache, every moment he had spent thrashing in his bed because he missed her with a bone-deep hunger.

On a beautiful October evening, he waited with his breath hovering in his throat while a hundred guests looked on.

Giannis's mansion and grounds had been decorated lavishly and he stood under an archway in the garden. Lilies in beautiful arrangements spread their fragrance while the sky glittered a brilliant blue.

Most of the guests had come to see his beautiful bride, the new designer that had shaken the fashion world with her designs—models she had worked with the past couple of months, half the population from his estate, workers from her factory, all because of Leah's generosity of spirit, her kindness, the depth of her commitment and loyalty.

And finally today, the magnificent woman was going to be his in a bond born out of love and laughter and joy. His heart ached as he remembered how much Calista would have loved to see Leah and him like this…

And there she was, on Dmitri's arm, walking toward him with sure steps.

His heart threatened to jump out of his chest when he saw her.

She had told him she was going to wear her own creation—the first wedding gown she had ever designed.

She looked utterly fragile and so beautiful that he stared hungrily, desire fisting tight in his gut.

Her long hair was combed away in a stylish ponytail, pearl earrings that had been a gift from Giannis at her ears, and the dress she wore was a demure creation in lace and sheer silk that didn't bare an ounce of flesh.

The modern, no-frill design hugged her slender body, leaving her arms bare, highlighting the long line of her thighs and legs.

Had she made the outfit more modest because of him? Did she think he wouldn't like it if it was one of her outrageously sexy, insubstantial creations?

Had he made her doubt his love again?

But one look into her gorgeous, shining eyes and all his doubts perished like so much dust.

They shone with such happiness that he felt a tightness in his chest relent.

They had spent the last three months touring for fabrics, laughing, and teasing each other, learning each other and falling in love all over again, and breathlessly waiting for this day.

He felt his entire world sway and tilt at the love he saw in those eyes, at the way her luscious mouth trembled.

She kissed Dmitri's cheek and he handed her over to him.

Gripping her fingers with his, he pulled her closer, the scent of her hitting him right in the solar plexus. "I love you, Leah," he whispered in her ear, without waiting for the priest to begin.

Her breath caught, she ran shaking fingers over his cheek as if she needed to check that he was all there.

"I can't wait for tonight," she finally whispered, and pulled back, a wicked twinkle in her eyes.

It was only later that Stavros finally noticed the back of Leah's dress. Specifically when the photographer had asked her to turn around and smile over her back.

Her gaze holding his, she turned slowly, a coy smile curving her mouth.

Heat pounded his blood, desire hitting him like a tsunami.

Her back was bare, dipping precariously low to the curve of her buttocks, except for a row of white buttons drawing a tempting line down her spine, holding the sheer illusion panel together…

Just the sight of that smooth, bare skin sent heat searing across his own.

He could love her for years to come but his wife would always surprise him, he realized with a smile.

Joining her, he ran his fingers up her spine, a fever overtaking his muscles.

"Ready for your wedding night, *yineka mou*?" he asked, pressing a kiss to her jaw.

She trembled and turned into his arms. "Do you like the dress?"

He nodded, and picked her up. A hundred cheers went up around them as he walked toward the entrance to Giannis's house. "I love it. But I apologize in advance."

Her hands tightened around his nape. "For what?"

"For ripping those delicate buttons. That's the only way to get it off you, isn't it?"

Her smile reached into the depths of his heart. He carried her over the threshold and took her mouth in a hungry kiss. "Now you're mine forever and forever."

"And you are mine," she whispered, before claiming his mouth again.

* * * * *

MILLS & BOON®

The Italians Collection!

2 BOOKS FREE!

Irresistibly Hot Italians

You'll soon be dreaming of Italy with this scorching six-book collection. Each book is filled with three seductive stories full of sexy Italian men! Plus, if you order the collection today, you'll receive two books free!

This offer is just too good to miss!

Order your complete collection today at
www.millsandboon.co.uk/italians

MILLS & BOON®

MODERN™

POWER, PASSION AND IRRESISTIBLE TEMPTATION

A sneak peek at next month's titles...

In stores from 21st August 2015:

- **The Greek Commands His Mistress** – Lynne Graham
- **Bound to the Warrior King** – Maisey Yates
- **Traded to the Desert Sheikh** – Caitlin Crews
- **Vows of Revenge** – Dani Collins

In stores from 4th September 2015:

- **A Pawn in the Playboy's Game** – Cathy Williams
- **Her Nine Month Confession** – Kim Lawrence
- **A Bride Worth Millions** – Chantelle Shaw
- **From One Night to Wife** – Rachael Thomas
